STAR WARS
THE LAST JEDI
COBALT SQUADRON

Written by
ELIZABETH WEIN

Illustrated by
PHIL NOTO

DISNEY
LUCASFILM
PRESS
LOS ANGELES · NEW YORK

For information address Disney • Lucasfilm Press,
1200 Grand Central Avenue, Glendale, California 91201.

Printed in the United States of America

First Hardcover Edition, December 2017

3 5 7 9 10 8 6 4 2

FAC-020093-17349

ISBN 978-1-368-00837-2

Library of Congress Control Number on file

Visit the official *Star Wars* website at: www.starwars.com.

SUSTAINABLE FORESTRY INITIATIVE   Certified Sourcing
www.sfiprogram.org
SFI-00993

THIS LABEL APPLIES TO TEXT STOCK

For my cousins in both generations.
May the Force be with you.

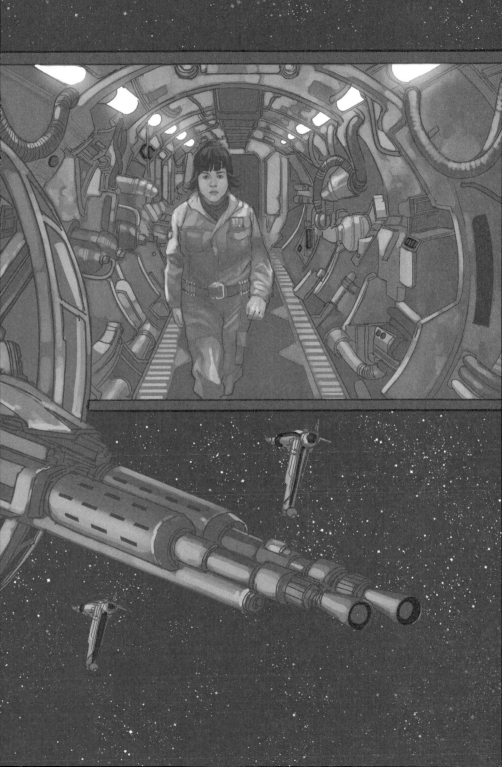

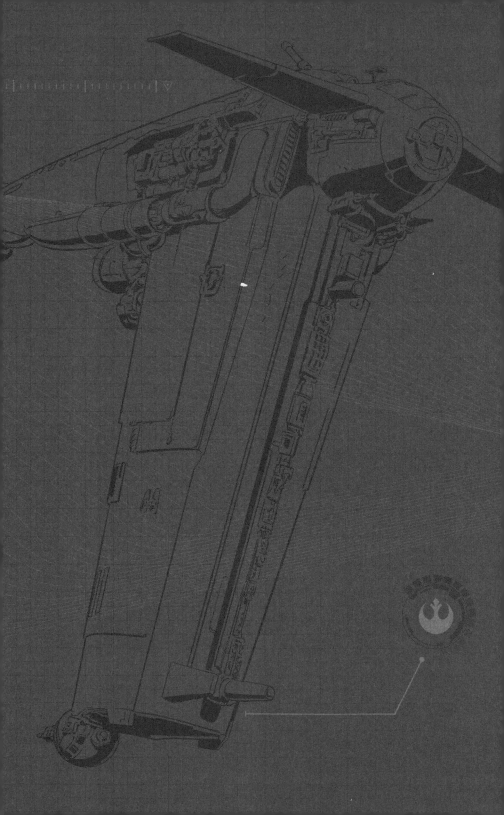

NOTHING, ROSE thought, *is as peaceful as the limitless blue of hyperspace.*

As soon as they jumped to lightspeed, she took off her safety straps. She made her way down the long access ladder past the dimly lit bomb racks to the gunner's ball turret, where her older sister, Paige, rode at the bottom of the heavy bomber ship.

Rose liked to join Paige in the lower turret when they were traveling in hyperspace. She often felt that the lightspeed travel during a mission was the only time she and Paige really had to themselves. Even though they were usually sent on the same assignments, it was rare that they were alone together.

"Nice to see you, Rose," Paige said as Rose settled alongside her sister. The crystal cage of the gunner's ball turret wasn't designed for more than one person to sit in it at a time, so Rose cozied up against Paige behind the laser cannon, practically sitting in her sister's lap.

"I can't stay long," Rose answered. "I need to keep an eye on the little monster I invented. I've got to make sure the power baffler is working the way it's supposed to."

"You sure it'll hide us? It's hard to miss a StarFortress."

"It's not supposed to *hide* us. It doesn't make us invisible. It just stops our energy trace from showing up on a sector scan. The baffler can't stop anyone from seeing us, but it might stop them from *noticing* us. And you know what happens if anyone notices us. . . ."

"Well, if they *do*, that's why I'm sitting here behind a laser cannon," Paige said.

Just for a little while, sitting safe in the clear cocoon of the gunner's turret with her older sister as they sailed through the suspended reality of lightspeed, Rose ought to have felt absolutely no fear.

Since the Tico sisters had fled the First Order's ruin of their home planet in the Otomok system and found their way to the Resistance base on D'Qar, there had always been something to worry about. From dark reports of First Order clampdowns in other star systems, to damaged ships that had to be rewired and armed *just in case*, to every now and then a wounded pilot's being hastily carried past on the way to the medbay, on D'Qar there were always reminders of reasons to be afraid. In hyperspace, there was nothing, and no reason to be afraid.

Really? Rose asked herself. *What about the past? What about the future?*

Even in these moments of calm, the fear was always there.

Rose remembered what had happened to her homeworld. The fear wouldn't go away until the First Order was completely destroyed. She didn't believe a word of the party line about bringing civilization to the far reaches of the galaxy. She'd seen what they did to the Otomok system: the ice sheets littered with the debris of the First Order's constant weapons testing and oily smoke rising from the poisoned settlements. At some point, other people were going to witness the chaotic horror that Rose and Paige had experienced. Rose was determined to put an end to it. She and her sister had joined General Leia Organa's Resistance movement with the full intention of bringing down the First Order.

In the quiet of hyperspace, Rose could wad her fear into a ball and temporarily jam it into a corner of her brain where she didn't have to think about it for an hour or so. But it was still there.

When Rose looked down through the clear crystal panes of the gunner's ball turret, she couldn't see anything but depthless mottled blue. But when she looked up, leaning back against Paige's shoulder in the swiveling seat suspended in the clear globe, she could see the massive hulk of the well-used heavy bomber *Hammer* towering ominously overhead.

"You're breathing hard," Paige said.

"That's because I've been getting some exercise," Rose said breezily. "That long climb past the bomb racks is as good as a workout."

That was true. But it hid the fact that Rose was scared. And Rose didn't want any of the crew to notice it, least of all Paige, who worried like crazy about Rose. They were the only family they had now—the only people they knew who'd made it out of the Otomok system.

Paige and Rose's homeworld, Hays Minor, and its sister planet, Hays Major, had spun just at the edge of what could be considered *habitable* in the Otomok system. Cold and dark, Hays Minor had been so far from the sun that its inhabitants had lived in perpetual twilight.

Now Paige mostly crewed *Hammer*'s guns, but she was trained as a pilot. Back home in Otomok she'd flown a stripped-down version of this MG-100 StarFortress bomber, blasting away the dark polar ice of Hays Minor for the Central Ridge Mining Company so the work crews could get at the surface of the planet. Paige's skill meant that now she could sometimes swap roles with Finch, *Hammer*'s pilot, or take over for him on long flights so he could get some sleep.

Rose couldn't remember a time when she and her sister hadn't shared a love of the sky. But then the First Order had filled the skies of Hays Minor with so much dust and filth that the Tico family could no longer see the stars from the observation dome of their living pod. Paige and Rose's desperate parents had managed to smuggle their children out of Otomok as refugees. Wearing filtered goggles because their eyes hadn't yet adjusted to the bright sunlight of an inner planet, with no clothes except those they'd traveled in, when Rose and Paige had met General Leia Organa for the first time, Paige had told her, "Our planet's being murdered."

Leia had answered seriously, "I understand."

Flying for the Resistance, Rose could see the stars again. But she couldn't ever go home.

"I don't like climbing the bomb racks when they're full," Paige said sympathetically. "Creepy, don't you think? All those black shining shells, every one of them full of explosives."

"Definitely creepy. Even now, when they're not full of bombs."

Instead, they were full of probe droids equipped for a quick and secretive spy mission.

Normally, *Hammer* operated as part of the Cobalt Squadron of Resistance heavy bombers. But this flight to the Atterra system was supposed to be a quiet fact-finding trip, and *Hammer* was on its own for once. The ship's bomb bays were filled not with destructive magno-charge explosives but with self-propelled probe droids that were too small to be detected on most routine scanners.

General Leia Organa wanted to find out the truth about what the First Order was doing to local settlements in Atterra. There were frightening rumors that traders who'd normally had no trouble getting in and out of the system were finding it blockaded. Armed ships were preventing access to Atterra's regular space routes. If anyone slipped past the guard ships, they were attacked by automatic cannons mounted on the Atterra system's many asteroids. The cannons were equipped with visual sensors that fired at anything that went near them. And at least one report mentioned deadly patrols of TIE fighters roaming Atterra's asteroid belt and the orbits of the Atterra system's twin inhabited planets.

Atterra was in a distant corner of First Order territory, but it had always been a safe place to trade. The First Order wasn't supposed to be attacking neutral shipping lanes with automatic cannons.

Otomok had been blockaded before it was destroyed, too.

Leia was one of the few people who suspected that the First Order was planning a bigger bid for power than was obvious. So she sent a single StarFortress heavy bomber to Atterra to do a little spying for her.

"I can't believe Atterra has twin planets and they're both inhabited," Rose said. "What are the chances! Just like home. It makes me want to *fight* for them."

"I know," Paige agreed. "Atterra Alpha and Atterra Bravo. I can't wait to see them. The general's got a soft heart, choosing us for this hop."

Of course, it wasn't entirely a soft heart that had made Leia choose Paige and Rose's ship to carry the probe droids to Atterra. Rose was good at coming up with make-shift solutions to technical problems. When she'd seen the mini spy-shields that helped camouflage the flight of the probes, she'd started wondering if there was a similar way to modify the engines and computers of her own ship. Rose's "little monster," the power baffler, was her quick-fix solution to disperse the energy emitted by the ship's power sources so it became undetectable except at close range.

Their current assignment was to fly into Atterra Bravo's orbit and release half of *Hammer*'s cargo of spy probes, then do the same with the rest of the probes over Atterra Alpha. They'd wait in the quiet starlight of space for a few hours while the droids flew over the surface of both planets, taking recordings and observations—and if they were lucky, not attracting any attention in the process. Then the heavy bomber would pick up all the satellite droids and fly back with their information to the Resistance base on D'Qar.

Paige and Rose and their crewmates didn't have any idea what kind of fate awaited them if they were discovered in orbit around Atterra Alpha and Atterra Bravo. Apart from the pilot's guns and the laser cannons in the turrets, they didn't have any way of fighting back if they were attacked. *Hammer* the StarFortress wasn't built for high speed or maneuverability; the ship was built to carry a thousand rocket-propelled shell cases. Normally, if it was going to engage in a battle, it would have an escort of fighter ships. Its load of bombs could be used for breaking ice in a mining operation or blowing up an enemy base— depending on whether its crew was at peace or at war.

In this strange middle ground between peace and war, it seemed there was another use for the heavy bomber: as a shuttle for a thousand electronic spies.

"It'd be nice to be able to live without being afraid," Paige said, reading Rose's mind.

"Who, me, scared?" Rose countered quickly. She tapped at Paige's medallion of pale gold Haysian ore, the teardrop shape of a snowgrape leaf, whose cord was wrapped tightly around the gunsight mount of the laser cannon. It usually hung around Paige's neck, but she liked to have it where she could see it during a mission. Rose had one almost exactly like it, hidden against her skin beneath her flight suit. The matching pendants fit together to make the ensign of the Otomok system, and it was the single physical link to their home planet that they still shared. Their parents had given them the medallions when they'd said good-bye. "We never really lived without fear, even at home, did we?" Rose pointed out.

"Maybe you don't remember living without fear," Paige said. "But I'm older than you. It was never *easy* living on Hays Minor, even before the First Order came. But until they arrived, kidnapping and killing, we weren't afraid. Mom and Dad weren't afraid until they started worrying about *us*."

Rose couldn't feel the shining medallion on the gunsight mount beneath her gloves. And she couldn't feel the one that lay against her skin any more than she could feel her undershirt or her socks—they were just *there*.

"Being afraid is like wearing my medallion," Rose grumbled. "It's part of me. I forget about it sometimes. But even when I'm not thinking about it, it's still there."

"Cheer up," Paige said. "So am I! Even when you're not thinking about me, I'm still here. We're in this together—whatever happens."

"Got to go," Rose said as her family time with Paige came to an end. "I'll be back for the trip home."

"See you then, Rose," Paige told her casually, as she always did before a bombing hop.

Rose climbed the long ladder back up to her place at the flight engineer's monitors to be ready for the moment they emerged from hyperspace and into the Atterra system.

Atterra was supposed to be a total nightmare for pilots to navigate.

Between the uninhabited giant Atterra Primo and the inhabited twin worlds of Atterra Alpha and Atterra Bravo, there were thousands of asteroids, all in orbit around Atterra's yellow sun. Many of these lumps of interplanetary rock were also in orbit around each other; tidal forces among them caused constant collisions.

Closer to the sun, just beyond this chaotic celestial parade, the planets Alpha and Bravo spun steadily on the same path in stable balance. They each had a single moon, and were far enough apart that they didn't influence each other's gravity. Both planets supported life.

It was a rare thing to find twin worlds within a star system's habitable zone. Atterra Alpha and Bravo weren't at all like Hays Minor and Major in terms of climate and terrain—but just the fact of the Atterra worlds being together in their orbit, like sisters, made Rose feel drawn to them. She *knew* how dependent those sister planets could be, so close together in the vast emptiness of space. She wanted badly for their future to be a happy one.

She couldn't wait to see them.

"Hey, Nix," Rose called when she neared the flight deck and could see the bombardier. Nix waved to her but didn't answer aloud. He was standing at his computer pedestal, busy counting off the probe droids in the bomb racks to make sure they were activated and ready for the drop when *Hammer* reached the orbit of Atterra Bravo.

Finch Dallow, the pilot, greeted Rose through the open bulkhead door as she strapped herself into her seat at the flight engineer's monitors. The heavy bomber wasn't built for luxury; its walls were rough and unfinished, with all the ducts and wiring laid bare. But the tech was up-to-date. "Ready for this?"

"Paige says it'd be nice to live without fear," Rose answered. "But I'm ready for anything."

She *was* ready for anything. She just didn't like always having to be in a constant state of readiness.

"Who wants to live without fear?" said Finch. All the crew members had their own burning reasons for joining the Resistance. Rose didn't know what Finch's was, or what nightmares he'd witnessed as a pilot for the New Republic scout service. He was relentlessly cheerful; it was good cover for whatever his real feelings were. He told Rose, "This'll be fun."

They suddenly emerged back into realspace on the edge of the Atterra system's gigantic asteroid belt.

Almost immediately, Finch threw the heavy bomber into a wild swerve and then a wild dodge in the other direction.

"What in the—" yelled Nix, hanging on to the bombardier's pedestal.

"Sorry—" Finch grunted. "Wasn't expecting reentry to be quite so close to that lump of rock."

He straightened out the ship. "Okay, Rose, if I promise to settle down, can you check and make sure the baffler's working?"

"I'm on it," Rose said, and quickly set the flight engineer's monitors to automatic. Then, still reeling from Finch's sudden swerve, she undid her straps to make her way to the cumbersome and makeshift machine that took up most of the space between the monitors and the tail gunner's turret high in the top of the ship.

The baffler was a complex half droid, half computer that Rose had rigged together to communicate with the ship's engines and randomly bleed off their ion exhaust. That way the ship's power scan looked like it was using hardly any energy, when the StarFortress was actually operating at full blast.

Rose had mixed feelings about this creation of hers. *Little* wasn't exactly the right word for her mechanical monster. It annoyed her that she hadn't been able to come up with a way to make it smaller. But she'd had to plug in a link to every single circuit in the engines, and there just wasn't room to do it in less space in the short time she'd been given to work on it. The similar tech on the probe droids in the bomb racks seemed so efficient. Of course, the probe droids were a lot smaller than the StarFortress to begin with.

But Rose was secretly very proud of how the baffler worked. She hadn't had a lot of time to put it together, and so far it had been doing its job very well.

"How's it going?" she asked it. "Is the ship talking to you the way it's supposed to?"

The baffler gave a responsive chirp. The massive machine was suspended from the top of *Hammer*'s fuselage, leaving a gap of less than half a meter above the flight deck. The gap was just wide enough to let Rose crawl inside the machine when she needed to reach the multiple plugs that connected to the engines. But it wasn't easy getting in, and Rose hesitated, wondering if she should check all the connections again.

As she stood there making her decision, a tremendous blast to the ship knocked Rose off her feet.

Automatically stubborn, she stood up while the ship was still rocking, and a second blast threw her across the flight deck headfirst into her own monitor station.

For a moment Rose was aware of nothing but the dazzling lights behind her closed eyes. Then she heard Finch's voice as the pilot checked on his crew through their headsets.

"Sorry, kids, that was two direct hits. Looks like automatic cannon fire from one of the asteroids—must have gotten too close for Rose's power baffler to confuse it. Took me by surprise. We're out of range now and the shields seem to have held—everybody okay?"

Rose's headset blocked the sound of the ship's engines, but with her hands flat on the floor of the metal flight deck beneath her body, she could feel the faint hum of power throbbing reliably against her palms. Everything was still working.

Paige spoke with her usual calm from the lower gun ball turret below the bomb bay. "All right down here. I guess General Leia's suspicions were right, as usual, huh?"

"Looks like it," said Finch. "Bombardier? You with us?"

"Hanging on for dear life and on target for surveillance," confirmed Nix. "That hit me halfway down the access ladder. Pretty happy I'm wearing these traction gloves." His voice wasn't as steady as Paige's as he answered Finch's roll call—no one's ever was—but Nix sounded determined, and if he'd been hurt he wasn't saying so.

It was a nasty shock to discover that there really were

defensive weapons mounted on the countless asteroids of the Atterra Belt.

"There's another of those blasted space rocks coming up at oh-two-oh—I don't know if it's armed or not. So brace yourselves," warned Finch. "Tech, how are you doing?"

Rose realized she was still lying facedown on the flight deck.

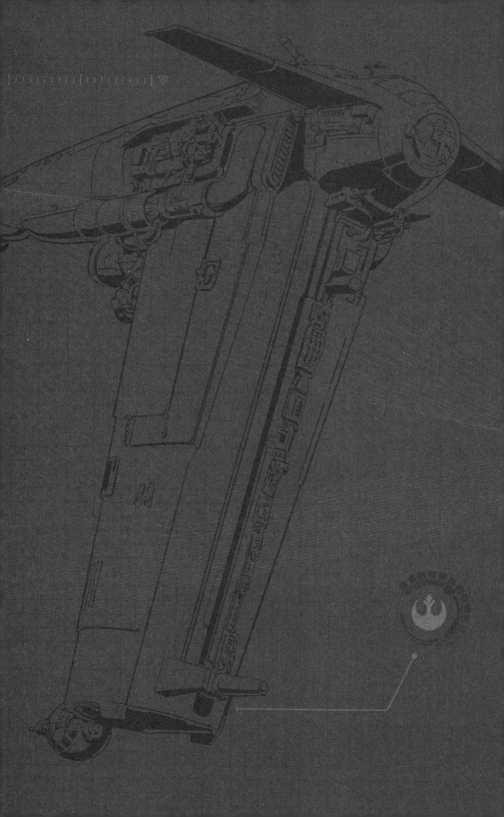

02

ROSE GRABBED for the edge of the chair that was locked in place in front of her flight engineer's monitors and pulled herself up so she was sitting on the floor.

She could see Finch up front in the cockpit. If he had turned around, he would have seen Rose sitting there, but he didn't dare look away from the flight path he was negotiating through Atterra's bizarre planetary system.

"I'm okay," Rose said shakily, and with another effort pulled herself back to her feet. She glanced at the tech screens. From her console in the ship's rough, windowless fuselage, there was no outside view except for what showed on the monitors. The images of Atterra's asteroids showed a navigator's nightmare, a dazzle of obstacles.

Rose repeated, "I'm okay!"

"Hey, that's *great* news," Finch said. "Because I need your help up here—the starboard rocket won't stop firing. I think it jammed when I kicked the links. It's wasting fuel we don't have and boosting the power that we're trying so hard to hide and plus—"

He paused to take a breath, and finished, "*Plus* it's trying to steer us straight into this blasted asteroid."

"Maybe you need a refresher in flight training." Rose kept her voice light as she made the lame joke. She knew Paige was listening, down in her fragile and exposed crystal sphere of a gunner's turret beneath the belly of the heavy bomber, and a lame joke would reassure Paige that Rose wasn't hurt.

Rose ran along the flight deck to the cockpit. *Hammer* wasn't built for a copilot, so there was only one fixed seat in the cockpit and no room for Rose except to stand behind Finch. From the clear egg-shaped dome of the pilot's canopy, Rose had a quick look at the real challenge Finch was facing.

It was almost like looking at the rush of starlight that you saw for a moment as you entered hyperspace. But the thousands of lights that glowed all around, as far as the eye could see, weren't stars; they were the asteroids of the Atterra Belt, lit not by their own energy but by the glow of their shared yellow sun. The farthest appeared as steady stars, those in the middle distance as glowing moons, and way too close for comfort, the nearest appeared to be a mountainous and barren globe of red rock looming above the StarFortress.

"What did you have to go and kick the activator links for?" Rose scolded.

"I didn't do it *on purpose*," Finch said defensively. "It happened when the cannons got us."

His guidance of the ship was featherlight even beneath his gloves, one finger hovering over the controls. He didn't look worried.

But Rose heard the strain in his voice when he said, "I can't let go of the ship. Can you get at the links if I put my feet up?"

"Cake," Rose said, as if it were going to be easy.

Finch raised his knees and wedged his boots up against the frame of the cockpit dome. He didn't look away from the view outside as he assumed the awkward position, or shift his hands a fraction from the controls.

Rose crawled underneath the pilot's seat. The panel that was supposed to protect the links for the rudder rockets was wedged inward as a result of the kick Finch had given it, obviously jamming the rockets into a permanent on position. It would have been an easy fix if Finch could have moved out of the way.

Rose managed to wedge a lever from her tool belt behind the jammed panel, but she couldn't get into the right position to apply enough force to loosen it.

"Put your right foot down," Rose said.

"Seriously? Like this?"

"Just like that." She took hold of Finch's boot and guided it to rest on top of the lever she'd wedged in position.

"Now kick down. Just like you did earlier."

"You want me to give it *another* kick?" Finch laughed without mirth. "Okay—"

He obeyed cautiously, his eyes on the myriad large and small asteroids ahead of him and the enormous one they were in immediate danger of crashing into.

"Not like that. Use the back of your heel—just one good firm kick," Rose said.

Finch kicked, and the stuck panel shot out of the wall with a clatter. Rose dodged the metal slab and Finch's descending boot. She scanned the rocket links, spotted the one that had been forced too far forward, and eased it back into place.

"Perfect!" Finch cheered. "Thank you! Was that so hard?"

Rose banged her headset against the bottom of the pilot's seat trying to get out.

"Ow! Does this ship hate me?"

She straightened up, holding on to the back of Finch's seat, and for a moment forgot her outrage. She just watched, riveted by the incredible unfeeling beauty of the glowing system.

Then she remembered why it might be dangerous.

"Be careful about getting close to those big asteroids,"

Rose warned the pilot. "The power baffler fails at close range. If there's anyone there, they'll be able to see us with their own eyes."

"We're back on track," Finch called to the rest of the crew. "Rose, take your seat in observation. Nix, map that automatic cannon on the asteroid we just passed, will you? Call it Atterra One-Seven-Oh-Six-Four. I don't want to trigger it a second time. It probably sends a firing report and if we go near it again, whoever put it there will start to get suspicious."

"Plus it might shoot at us again," came Paige's calm voice through Rose's headset.

"Cannon on Atterra One-Seven-Oh-Six-Four," Nix said. "Got it."

"Then get ready to release the probe droids," Finch added. "Atterra Bravo should be in range in ten."

"Counting," Rose heard Nix confirm through her headset.

———————

Rose's "observation" seat was the upper gun turret, high in the tail of the heavy bomber. Like Finch's guns and those in Paige's ball turret far below beneath the bomb bays, the guns in the tail turret were loaded just in case *Hammer* happened to encounter enemy fire.

Rose hoped she wouldn't have to use her guns. The

baffler might be able to hide the power from the ship's engine, but it couldn't disguise the power blast of laser fire.

She gave the baffler a fond pat as she squeezed past it to get to her observation post. The machine chirped at her in reply.

As Rose climbed into the seat in the clear crystal sphere of the tail turret, again she felt she'd been struck through the heart by the unimaginable beauty of Atterra's thousands of asteroids.

"Wow, what a view!" she exclaimed.

"This is what we wanted to see, right?" Paige's voice in Rose's headset was warm as she agreed with her younger sister. "Remember how we missed the stars when the First Order filled our sky with dust and warships? When we used to talk about seeing the galaxy together, it was for *this view*, right?"

"Sure, this is just like a luxury galactic vacation cruise," Rose joked.

But she had to admit it was beautiful. The asteroids were dazzling, lighting space all around like moons and stars, as far as the eye could see.

"A pilot's dream!" Paige added.

"Ha ha," said Finch, who was probably sweating. It had to be nerve-racking flying in this system. "Nix, the release is coming up in two. We're about to leave the belt. Then it's easy riding till we enter Atterra Bravo's inner orbit."

Paige and Rose, facing backward, hadn't been able to see the planet as they approached. But as Finch drew alongside Atterra Bravo to release the spy probes, their view changed.

Atterra Bravo was a world of pearly dark gold, seemingly glowing in the sunlight with that superficial serenity many worlds had from a distance. Even Rose's own cold and twilit home planet, Hays Minor, had had that serene glow when viewed from space.

"We're in the drop zone," Finch reported. "Release when ready."

"Bombs away!" called Nix exuberantly. Rose knew he'd been ready, with his finger on the remote trigger, the whole time she'd been fixing the rudder rockets.

From her seat high in the tail of the StarFortress, Rose couldn't see the bomb bay doors open. But she could see the probe droids as they jettisoned into Atterra Bravo's orbit—like a fine storm of dust swirling away from the ship and rapidly disappearing. They'd circle the planet over the course of the next eighteen hours or so, gathering data, and then the ship would go back to collect them.

In the meantime, the bomber would travel to the far side of Atterra's sun and visit Bravo's sister planet.

Rose's heart gave a little jump of excitement at the thought. *Just like home,* she thought. *So far, so good.*

"Bomb bay doors shut," Nix reported. "Ready for the next drop when you are, Captain."

"All right—we're on our way."

Then it was back out to the cover of the myriad asteroids and off to meet Atterra Alpha.

Rose watched the beautiful dark gold pearl of Atterra Bravo grow smaller behind her. She wouldn't be able to see its sister world, Atterra Alpha, until they were alongside it.

"Keep a good lookout," Finch said. "If the rumor is true that the First Order is policing traffic between the two Atterras, there are probably more of those guns."

He added ominously, "And we don't have any way of guessing where."

———

They flew steadily around the sun, dodging celestial bodies along the way, and made the next release at Atterra Alpha without meeting anything out of the ordinary.

Then they had to wait for the probes to do their work. Paige took over the pilot's controls for a while so Finch could get some rest.

The longer they waited, the more aware they became that the area wasn't as empty as it seemed.

Ships large and small appeared and disappeared on the monitors, blinking across the screen and winking out again. Some of them seemed to be in orbit around the two inhabited planets. Some of them appeared to be patrolling the complex belt of asteroids.

Rose wondered uneasily if they were looking for intruders.

If General Leia was right about Atterra being forcibly *blockaded*, then surely someone was trying to keep spy ships like the Resistance heavy bomber *Hammer out.*

Rose figured it was worth repeating what she'd told Paige earlier.

"The baffler mostly hides how much power we're giving off, but we can't stop anyone from seeing us with their own eyes," she reminded her sister through the comm system as Paige piloted the StarFortress. "If we hide behind something *big*, those ships are less likely to spot us. Get close to one of the asteroids if you can."

"You told Finch before *not* to get close."

Rose rolled her eyes and sighed. Of course no one could see her.

"Get close but not too close, okay? Not so close we attract another automatic cannon. Just stay in the same place for a while."

They were lucky. The asteroids did seem to hide the Resistance bomber; at least, no one *noticed* it. The baffler purred away, reliably doing its job to disguise their power emissions, and the dark side of the protective asteroid kept the light from glancing off *Hammer*'s reflective surfaces. For several hours the StarFortress lurked out of sight.

For a few minutes Rose actually slept, too, fitfully, lying back in the gunner's seat beneath the reflected light of the Atterra system's many asteroids.

Finch woke her when they were ready to gather up the spy probes. Rose had to be back at her flight engineer's monitors for that, because she was in charge of counting them in like a nerf herder while Nix, below in the open bomb bay, slotted the probe droids back into place in the bomb racks.

"I've got a little bad news," Finch said. "We're losing a lot of the probes. I had a look at their comm reports and the ones in the most distant orbital paths keep colliding with debris around both planets. Some of the probes activated their own self-destructs."

"What? Let me take a look."

Rose and Nix leaned over the monitors together, trying to tally the numbers. Because of their mini-baffler devices, the spy droids didn't show any trace of energy at all on the tracking screens. But every now and then one of them sent out a communications ping to let the bomber know it was doing its job. They were programmed to send out a "last word" if they exploded.

There was a growing list of last words.

Nix frowned. "I guess we were bound to lose a few."

"That's more than a few!" Rose exclaimed. "That's seven percent and climbing! They're supposed to act like droids, not a panicking nerf herd!"

"The ones we've lost were all in this outer ring at the edge of the planet's orbit," said Finch. "They're running into something. If there *is* a blockade in place—"

"*If?*" Rose repeated darkly, remembering the automatic cannons.

Finch ignored her sarcasm and continued, "If there's a blockade, this looks like part of it must include a mine-field around the planet's outer orbit. Maybe also further in. We'll have to be careful picking up the probes. We don't want to run into some kind of booby-trapped explosive device, either."

Hammer sailed out of hiding and back into orbit around Atterra Alpha, on track to intercept what remained of the first five hundred probe droids that had finished their spying sweep. The probes appeared on the monitors only as dots, lifeless as meteoroids. But they were all programmed to come home to the StarFortress, and Rose and Nix had to make sure they were all accounted for.

Paige and Rose spotted the first of the booby-trapped space mines at the same moment. Rose saw it as a sudden blossom of light on one of her monitors. Paige saw it through the crystal panes of the ball turret.

"There's a mine!" Paige cried out from the lower turret.

"You *see it?*" Finch said sharply. "Which way?"

"I didn't see it. I saw the explosion! One of the returning probes ran into it."

"Yeah, that one's gone," Rose said. The light on her screen had been the energy trace of the explosion. Now the doomed spy droid's final report flashed before her eyes.

"Look alive, kids," said Finch. "We're either in a minefield or we're right on the edge of it."

"I *do* see one!" said Paige. "Behind us, though—sort of silver. You can see them when the sunlight catches them. Smaller than a starfighter."

Sure enough, mines were scattered like jewels in a ring around Atterra Alpha, silent and shining and deadly. Although loaded with explosives, they weren't powered devices. They didn't emit any energy of their own. They just blew up if something ran into them.

Finch slowed the pace of the heavy bomber, looking. The pressure to spot the mines fell mostly on the pilot; Paige could see only behind the ship, and Rose and Nix couldn't see anything.

"I think we're outside them," Finch said. "We'd have hit one already otherwise."

"There's one!" yelled Paige. *"Underneath me.* You missed it by about ten meters."

Finch jinked, throwing the heavy bomber practically

on its side. When it was upright again he said shakily, "That was another."

"Should we get out?" Nix called.

"Can't," Finch said briefly. "Got to pick up the probes or we risk endangering the Resistance."

Rose counted them down as Finch flew cautiously.

But as the spy droids traveled in a steady stream back to their mother ship, Rose began to feel a bit more confident that the hop might actually be a success.

"Am I the only one who feels like we're a big old giant bait bird sitting out here in the open, waiting to gather up the baby birds while the predators close in on us?" Finch complained.

"Oh, stop moaning," said Paige in her matter-of-fact way. "No one's noticed us yet, and that's because we're *being careful not to be noticed.*"

"Yeah, listen to Paige and stop moaning," Rose called, then added with satisfaction, "That's all our baby birds from Atterra Alpha safely back in the nest. Let's get out of here."

"Okay, bombardier, close up those bomb bay doors and let's head back to Atterra Bravo to pick up the rest of our chicks," Finch commanded.

The flight back to Atterra Bravo didn't help reduce the crew's anxiety. They had to dodge no fewer than three other ships that appeared and disappeared from the monitors;

there was no way to tell if they were ordinary traffic or armed for the blockade. Instead of making swift progress to the pickup point, *Hammer* had to waste time hiding in the shadows of asteroids again. The craggy mountains of dark rock loomed like mountains. It was impossible not to imagine enemy ships hiding around every corner.

Then they had another nasty brush with an automatic cannon. But Finch saw it before they triggered its fire, and again swerved wildly away from it.

"I think I speak for us all," Nix announced, "when I say I will be very glad when we're back in open space."

"Roger that," Finch gasped, straightening the bomber's path.

Finally, they were in orbit again around Atterra Bravo, hoping not to run into another minefield.

But instead they ran into a new problem.

The first batch of spy droids they'd released had been out in the wild longer, and as a result they took more time to gather up.

The probes had spread out and were coming back to the ship in random groups—a handful at a time, sometimes only one or two, never more than a dozen together. Counting them in took longer than anyone had calculated.

"Eight just got back safe and sound," Nix called up to Rose from the bomb racks. "Can you see any more of them?"

"Here comes another bunch completing an orbit," Rose reported from the monitors. "Looks like six or seven, but it might just be space garbage—get ready in case they're ours. My gosh, it's *worse* than nerf herding."

She didn't actually know what nerf herding was like. But it couldn't be as bad as this.

"How many are still out there?" Finch called.

"After we scoop up this next bunch—*if* these belong to us—there's still another fifty or so to grab," Rose said. "Not counting the ones that have already blown up."

"Okay, nearly there," Finch said encouragingly.

It was at that moment that a strange dazzle of light appeared on the screen Rose was watching, as if someone had thrown a handful of illuminated snow crystals across the monitor.

And just as if the crystals had instantly melted, they swept in a line across the upper corner of her screen and vanished.

It looked like a squadron of starfighters.

03

ROSE BLINKED HARD. She stared at the screen, wondering if she'd imagined it—or if her tired eyes were fooling her.

As she gazed, wide-eyed, two of the gleaming pinpricks swept teasingly back into the upper corner and out of sight again.

"Um, Finch," Rose called, "I don't want to scare anybody, but I think there are a bunch of small ships out there—ahead of us, zero-one-three sector oh-nine, moving. They're out of range now but not *far* out of range. Look for them when they move—you'll see the sunlight on them."

She added, "Paige, keep your eyes peeled, but I don't think you can see them from the lower turret—they're ahead of us and high."

There was a long, heavy silence while Rose continued to tally the probe droids and Nix continued to shunt them back into the racks.

Then Finch suddenly said, "Got 'em. I mean, I see your bunch of ships, Rose—there are seven of 'em. In formation. They're sort of scanning back and forth across that sector—must be some kind of patrol. Could be bandits."

He meant an enemy, anyone who might attack them.

The pilot paused.

"How many of the droids are we missing?" he asked at last.

Rose checked the list. "Only seven left. They're just completing an orbit. If we sit here and wait for them, those patrol ships might see us. . . ."

Nix called up, "If we go hide in the asteroid maze again, we'll miss the rendezvous with the probes and have to wait an hour and a half for them to make another orbit."

"Or we could turn the engines on and go meet them now," Paige offered in her calm voice.

Finch gave a quick and bitter laugh. As if that weren't the most dangerous option available—the option that most risked the StarFortress getting noticed by the patrol of speedy ships that were zigzagging in and out of the top of Rose's screen and Finch's field of vision.

"Might as well get it over with," said Finch. "Nix— Rose—are you in?"

"Always willing to get it over with," said Nix. "I'm in."

Rose sighed audibly over everybody's headset. "Yeah, whatever Paige says."

"Ready for anything, right? Cool. Let me know what those speedy little patrol guys are up to, Rose," Finch said. "You've got the best view of them."

"Let *me* know if you need help getting rid of them," Rose said. From the flight monitors, she could keep an eye on what the patrol ships were doing, but she'd have to get into the tail gunner's turret if she needed to shoot at them.

———

"That's all but the last three probes in," Nix announced.

Rose's attention was still riveted to her screens.

She was beginning to see a pattern to what the patrol of small ships was doing, and she wasn't sure she liked it.

She was also itching to check on the baffler to make sure it was doing its job. She didn't like to think what might happen if the speedy ships that glittered across her screens were to notice the Resistance StarFortress sailing quietly along in Atterra Bravo's orbit, scooping up data-gathering spy droids full of information about what was going on at the planet's surface.

"Finch, when we've picked up all the probes, head straight back into the asteroid maze," Rose said.

"Got it," Finch said. Rose couldn't hear any nervousness in his tone, but she guessed he had to be coming to the same conclusion that she was about the patrol. And it was getting closer and brighter all the time.

The patrol was chasing someone.

The starfighters were growing near enough that if their pilots had been able to take the time to look, they'd have easily spotted sunlight glinting off the heavy bomber, even if its power trace wasn't visible.

But they were obviously focused on something else.

They weren't just routinely tracking back and forth; they were dodging and weaving, their formation breaking and reforming, following a glint of sunlight that streaked ahead of them.

The leading light wasn't part of the rest of the formation. The sparkle on the screen that led the handful of moving stars wasn't following the same pattern as the others. It was racing ahead, jinking wildly backward, and then somersaulting suddenly up or down when its path was cut off by one of the other lights.

It was trying to escape.

"How are we doing, Nix?" Finch called anxiously, because the dogfight, or whatever it was, was getting dangerously close. On its current path, *Hammer* was heading directly into the fray. "Aren't those probes in yet?"

"One left. *One left.*"

"Is it in range?"

"Not yet—"

"Can we just *leave it*? It'll run into one of those mines eventually and blow itself up."

Rose gritted her teeth. "Or maybe we could activate its self-destruct . . ."

If any of the probes were caught with the information they now carried, it would raise diplomatic questions that could have huge consequences in the New Republic Senate. Who'd sent the spy probes, and why? They were in First Order territory without authorization. The First Order could claim some kind of treaty violation, and Leia's case against them could be ruined.

Paige reminded the rest of the crew, "If Nix activates that probe's self-destruct now, the explosion guarantees we'll get the attention of those ships. It was probably the exploding mines that brought the patrol out here."

If the Resistance bomber were caught, now carrying nearly a thousand times the cargo of information that a single probe droid carried, they'd have to blow *themselves* up.

Finch sped with determination toward the last probe, and also toward the strange ships. With each second it seemed more likely that they were going to have to engage with them.

"Here comes that droid!" Rose yelled. "Nix, you ready?"

She stared at the screen. She could tell the droid by its shape. The other ships, closer now, were also beginning to show distinct outlines on the monitor.

Finch, watching the ships at a distance from the pilot's

cockpit, couldn't see the fine detail that Rose was able to zoom in on.

She called a warning in a low voice.

"They're TIE fighters. The patrol. *They're First Order TIE fighters.*"

"Thanks for the good news," said Finch. "All of them?"

"I don't recognize the shape of the thing they're chasing. It's like a tube. But tiny—some kind of starfighter? Even smaller than a TIE."

"Doesn't look like he's going to shake them, though," Finch observed.

"Can we pick up our cargo and get the heck out of here?" Paige called up.

"*Wise words from the lower gun turret,*" Rose called back.

"Closing on the last probe now," said Finch. "Nix, let me know as soon as it's in. I'm going to make a sharp turn out into the belt to get behind those asteroids while I initiate the lightspeed sequence. Then tell me the second the bomb bay doors are shut, because we can't enter hyperspace until they're closed."

"Understood," said Nix.

"Rose," Finch continued, "take your place in the tail gun turret—just in case."

Rose left the monitors and squeezed her way to the tail guns back past the baffler. The big machine hummed steadily. But Rose knew it couldn't hide them if they were seen.

She settled behind the laser cannon with her hands on the controls.

"Paige?" Rose said.

"I'm flying with you," her sister answered from below.

Facing back the way they'd come, Rose couldn't see what was going on as the last of the Atterra Bravo probes sailed home and Nix locked it in place.

"Let's go," came Nix's call, and Finch veered the StarFortress away from the planet's inner orbit and the sun.

The rockets blazed as Finch used full power. The moment they were flying perpendicular to the planet, Rose suddenly had a good view of the ships they'd been trying to avoid.

The TIE fighters were racing toward Atterra Bravo, all six flying in formation. Mostly they just appeared as speeding balls of light as the sun caught their surfaces, but for a split second they came close enough that Rose could see their distinctive shapes before they wheeled away again after their prey.

Rose began to hope that, if the TIE pilots had seen *Hammer* and its payload of spy droids, they were assuming it was part of their own blockade. They certainly weren't paying any attention to it; they were completely focused on the desperate ship they were pursuing.

Then, suddenly, all the hunting ships soared upward toward the heavy bomber.

"Are those doors shut yet?" Finch yelled.

"Not yet—I'm on it!" Nix yelled back.

Rose didn't dare fire at the TIE fighters. If they hadn't already noticed *Hammer* themselves, she sure wasn't going to attract their attention, not when they were so close to entering lightspeed.

What would Paige do? Rose asked herself.

Down below, Paige wasn't firing, either. Rose was sure she was doing the right thing. *Don't attack,* she told herself. *Defend yourself if you have to, but don't attack.*

Rose waited breathlessly as the seconds dragged by and the hunt grew nearer.

Just as the shadowy pockmarked surface of the nearest asteroid in the Atterra Belt obscured the view of space beyond the StarFortress, Rose saw the tiny ship that was the TIE fighters' prey. For most of the chase, it had appeared as nothing but a wayward and desperate pinpoint of light drawing acrobatic spirals in its effort to escape the TIEs. But now it made another quick turn away from its pursuers and streaked like a comet straight toward the Resistance bomber.

Simultaneously, Rose and Paige yelled warnings.

"Finch, behind you!"

"Nix, close the doors!"

"I'm trying!" Nix called. "We're moving at full power and it slows their operational speed!"

Rose's hands gripped the controls of her laser cannons. The fleeing ship's path as it sped toward her was a twisted corkscrew of feints and dodges—expert flying that was almost impossible to fix in her gunsight.

"Paige, can you nail him?"

"I don't—" The hesitation in Paige's voice was urgent, and held something Rose couldn't quite identify. And then Paige yelled again, without her usual calm, *"Are the doors closed?"*

Nix swore. *"Give me a few more seconds—"*

Rose knew what was holding Paige back. It was obvious the fleeing ship wasn't armed. It had never tried to fight back. It was just trying desperately to get away, and Paige didn't want to shoot at it. She didn't want to fire on a defenseless ship that was clearly trying to escape from a patrol of armed starfighters.

The little ship abruptly slowed as it closed in on *Hammer.* Rose took careful aim and held the craft in her gunsight. She got a good look at it—a worn and battered interplanetary starfighter of an unfamiliar design, slim and slender as a duct tube and just big enough to seat two people back-to-back with their legs straight out in front of them.

But Rose didn't fire. Paige wasn't firing in the ball turret below her, and that made Rose hold off also.

Suddenly, the strange ship put on a brief burst of speed, and a second later vanished beneath Rose's line of sight. And a split second after that, there was a tremendous crash and a thud that rocked the entire bomber.

A stream of obscenities from Nix poured into Rose's headset.

"What just happened?" yelled Finch.

"That crazy starfighter boarded us!" Paige yelled, all sign of her usual cool gone. *"They flew straight into the bomb bay!"*

"Nix?" cried Finch as he guided the heavy bomber at top speed into the maze of asteroids that circled Atterra's sun.

The bombardier was shaken, but answered the call: "I'm okay. Ship's okay. Doors shut. Good thing we aren't carrying real bombs! Looks like we've got a hitchhiker."

The TIE fighters came screaming after them, laser cannons blasting. Rose stopped worrying about whether or not firing back was the right thing to do. She leaned into the gun controls in the tail turret and fired. It was a *relief* to be doing something after all that waiting. Below her, the light of Paige's cannon fire paralleled her own. As if in a dream, without really paying attention to what they were saying, Rose heard Nix and Finch shouting at each other through the comm headsets.

"Doors are shut, you said?" That was Finch. "Everybody strap in for lightspeed—the second we're clear of these asteroids I'm going to jump."

"Um, is there something wrong with your headset, flyboy?" Nix growled furiously. *"We've got a hitchhiker."*

"And we've got a bunch of First Order TIE fighters on our tail," Finch snarled back. "Strap yourself in and get out your blaster and we'll deal with the stowaway when we're safe in hyperspace."

And with that, Finch left the Atterra Belt. The view around Rose in the crystal sphere of the tail gunner's turret sparkled with the light of the jump to lightspeed.

So much for the limitless peace of hyperspace, thought Rose.

Finch's deadpan drawl came through Rose's headset: "That was *not* standard galactic intercept procedure." She could hear him panting with the effort it must have taken to fly at full power through the maze of asteroids. "Rose, get down there and give Nix and Paige some backup."

Rose scrambled out of the tail turret and ran back to the access ladder that led down through the bomb bay.

Finch swung around on his chair to hail her. "Here, take one of my blasters. I'm just setting up the autopilot—I'll be right behind you."

Rose started down the ladder with Finch's blaster tucked into her tool belt.

She couldn't help looking down as she climbed.

Far below her, she could see the slender little starfighter wedged almost upright against the bomb racks in the foot of the StarFortress. One of the supports for the lower catwalk had twisted itself around the nose of the starfighter as it came to a sudden stop in a very small space that really wasn't designed to contain a ship. Several of the probe droids had been crushed in the impact.

Rose was halfway down the ladder when one of the twin canopies of the small starfighter began to open. She paused, double-checked her footing, and took aim with Finch's blaster *just in case*.

Finch paused on the ladder above Rose. Nix stood on the damaged lower catwalk, and Paige crouched by the hatch to her gun turret. Both of them had blasters raised.

Hammer's crew held their breath as they waited to see whom they'd caught.

The figure who climbed out of the cockpit was short and slender. The fugitive took a quick look around, saw

Paige and Nix with their threatening blasters, and held up gloved hands in surrender. Looking higher, the intruder saw Rose and Finch and gave a sort of despairing shrug.

Finch dialed in the universal comm on his headset. "Can you hear me?"

The other pilot didn't answer aloud at first—just gave a frightened nod. Then, speaking in a rush, the fugitive pointed to the other cockpit, whose inhabitant was struggling to get the canopy open from the craft's awkward wedged position. "I need to get her out—let me help her out!"

It was a youthful voice, a boy's voice, and it caught with emotion that nearly stopped the boy from finishing his sentence. Rose recognized that catch. It was connected to the reaction you had at the end of a battle—when you hoped you were safe again, for the time being, and your hands started to shake and your limbs felt like they were full of hot water.

"You can help her out if you don't try any funny business," Finch told him.

Nix climbed a little way up the ladder to get out of the way. Paige covered the young pilot with her weapon as he struggled awkwardly with the other canopy and finally managed to pry it up.

There was barely room for the starfighter's second occupant to crawl out. Paige finally put down her blaster and held out her hands so the stranger could hang on to her and pull.

"Ma'am? Are you all right?" the pilot cried, frantically trying to fight his way past the wedged ship to get to his passenger.

"I'm fine, boy," said the other, an older woman whose voice was breathless but practical. "Settle down. Don't scare anyone who's pointing a blaster at you."

Rose lifted her eyebrows in disbelief. She'd expected hostility—or, at the least, fear. This woman sounded like nothing could surprise her.

"Where are you headed?" Finch asked, with deadpan politeness.

"Out," the woman said. "Out of Atterra."

"So you'll be okay with us just dropping you off at the nearest spaceport, right?"

Her young pilot turned on Finch, nearly weeping with frustration. "You'd take us seriously if we were pirates, wouldn't you? Where were *you* headed?"

"Reeve," the woman cautioned in a pained voice.

"You're pretty unconvincing pirates," Rose couldn't help commenting. The boy sounded *scared.*

There was an awkward silence.

"Well, you're on our ship," Finch pointed out. "So either we're going to have to drop you off somewhere, or you'll have to come with us. I'm not going out of my way for you."

"No." The woman drew a deep breath. "No, no one's going out of their way for us. That's why we had to get out—"

"To tell the galaxy our planet's being murdered," the young pilot finished passionately.

Suddenly, Rose shivered, and Paige glanced up at her.

Those had been Paige's *exact words* to General Leia Organa the first time they'd met.

Paige swallowed. Then she remarked with careful calm, "That sounds important."

Finch nodded, and didn't take it any further for the moment.

Instead, he pointed upward, toward the opening above the bomb racks.

"You can't hang around here for the rest of the trip," he told the intruders. "Gonna have to make you both climb up to the flight deck. Are you up to it?"

"Doesn't look like we have much choice," said the imperturbable woman. "Lead the way. And . . ."

Now her voice shook just a little, as the relief of the daring escape caught up with her and the adrenaline subsided.

"And—*thank you*," she added, her voice suddenly fierce with emotion.

04

"SO WHAT do we do with them?" Finch asked his crew.

He'd switched the crew's comms back to their own channel so the intruders couldn't listen in. Exhausted and apprehensive, the hitchhikers sat on the floor of the flight deck facing each other. They didn't speak; they were obviously being cautious about whatever it was they were running away from.

"Take them back to base, fix their ship, wipe their flight computer, send them off to wherever they were headed. . . ." Nix trailed off. "Yeah, I can see why this is a problem. We can't let them know about the Resistance. Anyway, where *were* they headed? Did they think they were going to turn up on the doorstep of the Senate and get a hearing?"

With the hyperspace coordinates set for D'Qar, there weren't many options for getting rid of the stowaways before the bomber got back to the Resistance base. The Ileenium system was obscure even in the Outer Rim, and

General Leia Organa's secret stronghold certainly wasn't labeled on any star charts.

"Well, unless we drop them off somewhere on the way, they're going to find out about the Resistance when we get back, aren't they?" Finch countered.

"If they're on the run from the First Order they're not so different from me and Paige," Rose said. She glanced over her shoulder at the exhausted pair that sat slumped against the unfinished walls of the StarFortress. Both strangers seemed to be watching with suspicion and something like despair as the ship's crew discussed their fate. Rose asked, "What do you think, Paige?"

"I think they're probably *exactly* like us," Paige agreed. "So we should turn them over to Leia and let her deal with the situation herself."

Rose caught the refugees looking at her and waved, giving them a wide, bright smile that somehow felt fake on her own face. "Leia wanted us to bring her intelligence from Atterra, right? Well, we're bringing it—intelligent life!"

Nix and Finch laughed hollowly. Paige did not laugh.

Hammer came out of hyperspace on the far side of the planetary ring that circled D'Qar.

"This seems like a piece of cake after the Atterra Belt,"

Finch quipped. "Just fly under it. Remind me, next time I complain, that asteroids orbiting a planet are easier to navigate than asteroids orbiting a sun."

But he stopped wisecracking, because the last moments of the mission were busy as the complicated business of bringing the StarFortress in to land got under way. At a big space wharf, this was a straightforward maneuver. But the secrecy around D'Qar meant that at the end of each hop the massive, awkward StarFortresses had to be delicately guided over kilometers of treetops to the camouflaged bunkers of the Resistance base, then eased into makeshift underground docking bays where the bomb clips could be removed and replaced, just like the ammunition clips in some types of handheld blasters.

Nix stood guard over the strangers while the rest of the crew worked through the docking sequence. Paige monitored the tech screens while Rose shut down the baffler.

"Thanks for your guidance," Finch called through the comm to the ground crew team who'd worked to marshal *Hammer* into position and lock the ship in place.

Then he added with relish, "Prepare to receive prisoners."

Finch set the power to standby and took off his headset. He turned around to look at the waiting intruders.

"I've always wanted to say that," he told them, grinning.

One by one, the passengers in the heavy bomber

emerged from the flight deck onto the gantry above the floor of the bunker, with the crew flanking their "prisoners."

By the time they'd climbed down the ladders to the ground, a small crowd had gathered to watch. Nix gave the youthful pilot of the runaway starfighter a slight push between the shoulders so that he was forced to step forward into a circle of waiting soldiers. The boy threw an anxious glance over his shoulder at his companion.

The older woman was calmly taking her helmet off. Her short-cropped, iron-gray hair and hard, lined face gave her the look of a battle-worn commander.

Paige pulled off her own helmet and her gloves, and hung them by their straps over her shoulder. She said in an undertone to Rose, "We're in luck—Fossil's here."

Fossil was the commanding officer of the Resistance StarFortress unit that included the two squadrons Cobalt and Crimson. She stepped forward to stand in front of the guards and marshals and curious onlookers. Fossil was a Martigrade, a darkly eloquent and eerily sluglike silver-skinned biped; she was too large to go along as flight crew, but she managed to keep the entire team's every operational mission log and ship maintenance lists somewhere inside a head as big as Rose's torso. The bomber crews called her "the Old Lady" behind her back—but not to her stern and expressionless face. Until you knew her—and if you angered her—she was terrifying.

Fossil came forward now to face the two strangers. The young pilot froze when he saw her and took a fearful step backward.

Rose, watching, wondered why he was on this mission. He seemed much too easily frightened to have been sent out by his people as part of a rescue team. Rose whispered to Paige, "He's scared of Fossil."

But the other stranger, the tall gray-haired woman, took a step forward. Rose saw that her fearlessness made the young pilot straighten up a little.

Fossil said in her formal, ringing voice, "Take off your helmet, boy. I want to see your eyes."

"Here they are," he answered, obeying quickly. He flashed Fossil a bright, defiant smile. Rose thought he might be angry at himself for being scared.

She knew that feeling all too well. She recognized his desperate attempt to cover it with humor.

Facing the Martigrade, the gray-haired woman's shoulders rose and fell as she let out a sharp breath through flared nostrils.

"I understand why you can't immediately trust us, or take me at my word," she said to Fossil. "But go ahead and search our ship if you think it'll tell you more."

She waved a dismissive hand back toward the heavy bomber, which still held the little starfighter wedged in its bomb bay.

"We haven't brought anything with us. Not even ammunition—we haven't got any. Our guns have been stripped. Everything I've brought with me is in here"—the stranger tapped her head—"and here." She laid her hand on the trembling boy's shoulder. There was a dignity about her that commanded respect.

"Continue," Fossil invited.

"Where are we?" the strange woman asked.

"Where do you hope to be?" Fossil countered.

"I'm trying to reach one of the New Republic seats of government," said the stranger carefully. "I'm the district representative of the Firestone Islands on Atterra Bravo, which is in the jurisdiction of the First Order. I want to speak to someone with a voice in the New Republic Senate."

"I am not at liberty to tell you where you are," said Fossil.

The boy broke in, with desperation in his voice, "Look, couldn't you just tell us where to go next? This is the *fifth time* this season the Atterra system has tried to get someone past the blockade with news of how our people are being *murdered*—"

"Shhhh," his older companion said soothingly.

"And we're the only ones who haven't *died* in the attempt!" the boy burst out. "They *should* know. They need to know what's happening there!"

Fossil took a step closer. The young pilot stood his ground, quivering.

"Tell me," the huge sluglike Martigrade said gently. "I *want* to know."

"They're tearing apart our planet," said the boy simply, "and killing thousands of us every day." There was a fierce intensity to his voice that kept everyone quiet. He hadn't dared to look at Fossil since that defiant moment when she'd demanded to see his eyes. He wasn't brave enough to look at her. But he kept on talking. "When we try to send for help, our ships are shot out of the sky. Without help, two worlds are going down in flames."

Rose was fairly sure that nothing would delight Fossil more than to bring General Leia Organa fresh news of some concrete First Order atrocity—something Leia could use to build her argument with the New Republic for action against them.

But the Old Lady wasn't going to give away their game so easily.

"If I could make such a meeting happen for you," Fossil continued slowly, "*if* I could . . . I would need a very good reason for it. Can you give me one?"

The older woman looked at Fossil shrewdly, taking in the Martigrade commander's oversized head and crystalline eyes, each the size of a human palm.

"Here's one reason," said the tall gray-haired woman.

"Because your own people were persecuted by the old Empire long before the First Order claimed territory in our Atterra. You're one of those who've never given up fighting tyranny."

Fossil made a sound that everyone under her command knew meant, more or less, *I'll be the judge of that.*

But she raised one gigantic silver limb and motioned that the troops should let the two strangers proceed ahead of her.

"Bomber crew, come along," Fossil ordered. "We'll see what General Organa thinks of their story. Mission debriefing can wait."

Paige gave Rose a sideways glance, raising her eyebrows. Rose returned the same look, and Paige smiled. They fell into line behind Finch and Nix to follow Fossil and the crew of the strange ship into Resistance Headquarters.

———

Over her shoulder, General Leia Organa called to the attendant soldiers who'd escorted the refugees into the small map room. Her own guards stood behind her, alert and interested. "Did anybody think about getting these two something to eat and drink?" Leia asked.

"I'll go," volunteered one of the guards.

Leia faced the gray-haired woman for a moment without speaking, sizing her up. The general was considerably shorter than both the stowaways, but so fully sure of her own authority that her presence always seemed enormous.

Leia asked the strange woman mildly, "Who are you?"

As before, if the stranger was afraid, she didn't show it. Her young companion stood by her side, failing to imitate her calm control.

The woman said, "I'm Casca Panzoro, and this is Reeve Panzoro. He's my grandson; I needed a pilot and a ship to get me here. Reeve had to steal one."

"You're from Atterra Bravo?" Leia repeated. "They used to call it 'Free Atterra' during the rule of the Empire, didn't they?"

"That's right," said Casca Panzoro steadily. "We are a system of twin worlds, dependent on each other. Our sister planet, Atterra Alpha, was turned into a prison during the last years of the Empire. Bravo was free, but it was a time of living nightmare for both planets. Bravo's oceans are acidic, and Alpha's our only natural source for drinkable water, so when communication stops between our worlds, people on Atterra Bravo die of thirst more quickly than they starve."

"Fossil, pull up a map for us," Leia ordered.

The bomber unit's commander swept one of her three large silver-sheened digits over the console, and a hologram of the Atterra system blinked to life in the center of the room.

Paige and Rose glanced at each other. Rose knew that they'd both felt the same twinge of emotion when the desperate woman had spoken those familiar words: *twin worlds.*

Casca continued to speak steadily. "Twin worlds," she repeated, gazing at the star map. "Atterra Alpha and Atterra Bravo, in the Atterra system on the Outer Rim."

The hologram glowed, the miniature sister planets and other celestial bodies rotating rapidly around their small sun. It wasn't really like Paige and Rose's home system of Otomok. There was Atterra Primo, a giant planet whose gravity was too intense for human habitation, and between that and the twin Atterra worlds was the complex asteroid belt. Atterra Alpha and Atterra Bravo were much closer to their sun than the Hays planets had been in Otomok.

They must be so light and warm on the surface, Rose thought. She felt envious and protective at the same time.

Casca Panzoro glanced sharply around her, assessing how seriously people were taking her. *Hammer's* crew was listening intently. Leia's expression was of concern, but Rose knew that Leia was just as capable of being sneaky as any First Order spy. Fossil's vast features were always impossible to read.

Casca plunged on, the edge of defiance in her voice a little stronger now. It revealed the family resemblance she shared with her grandson.

"We were all right for a while after the Empire was defeated. But now the First Order is worse than the Empire. They're ravaging Atterra," Casca said. "They've imposed a blockade on us while they plunder our gas and minerals, and they're killing us as they do it. We can't get any supplies from outside the system, and we're forbidden to travel between our own planets. The First Order won't even let settlements on the same planet communicate with one another. We can't launch our own defense without fuel, and without being able to trade, people on both planets are starving.

"But it's worse on Atterra Bravo, where there's no natural source of fresh water. Even without being blockaded we can't produce enough water for people to stay hydrated in the tropical regions. Our people are dying of thirst."

Leia guessed, "So you want to make a complaint to the New Republic, behind the First Order's back?"

"Oh, starry seas, you'd take us more seriously if we *were* pirates," the young pilot Reeve Panzoro interrupted with uncontrolled frustration. "Isn't it obvious Ms. Casca's trying to get help from the New Republic? Who else would help her?"

Casca didn't scold the boy for interrupting. She said proudly, "It's true we need help. But we're not asking anyone to fight our battle for us."

"Well, what are you asking?" countered Leia.

Casca spoke plainly now, desperate enough to take a risk.

"I know the Senate is sympathetic to independent former Imperial colonies. We need supplies. If we could get them unofficially, then it wouldn't cause problems between the New Republic and the First Order. I understand why the Senate won't interfere—I know they don't want another galactic war. I know they can't take official action. But maybe if we kept it quiet . . . maybe if someone who'd been part of the old Rebel Alliance knew about us . . . or some private citizen with an interest in free trade. . . . If we had the ability to fight our own battle, the First Order might think twice about doing this again somewhere else. They've *got* to be stopped. Because if they get away with it in Atterra, they *will* do it somewhere else."

Rose saw that Paige was nodding grimly in agreement. Casca Panzoro didn't know it, but the First Order had already done it somewhere else.

The Atterran refugee was right: the First Order had to be stopped.

Casca hesitated before she continued to speak. Then she took a deep breath and plunged on.

"I told your lieutenant here that I'm the district representative of the Firestone Islands. What I didn't say is that I'm also the commander of a united resistance movement on Atterra Bravo. We call ourselves Bravo Rising.

We've managed to pull together a small fleet of starfighters and transport ships, and we've been making supply runs between our planets. We're capable of fighting back on our own."

Casca and her grandson, Reeve, suddenly met each other's eyes and exchanged a private, reassuring nod confirming their teamwork.

"But as I said, we do need help," Casca added. She paused to draw breath, and continued steadily, "We need fuel, and food, and weapons, and medical equipment. Access to water. Just enough to keep us going—enough that we can launch our own attack. The First Order ships in our skies aren't there legally—at least, it's their own territory, but they're not supposed to be starving and executing people in their own territory! We want to arm ourselves so we can survive."

Casca had finished her plea. There were a few moments of still silence, and the only things in the room that seemed to move were the circling planets of the hologram map.

Everything Casca Panzoro had said confirmed Leia's worst fears about Atterra—and about the First Order.

Leia reminded her neutrally, "You said you'd stolen your ship."

"Some of Atterra Bravo's settlements had their own security forces. Local organizations that used to police piracy and smuggling. The First Order has impounded all their ships, but we managed to hide some of them first. Reeve took his father's ship. His father—Rendal Panzoro, my son—was one of the pilots for the Firestone Islands Guards. They were brutally targeted by the First Order blockade—brutally and ruthlessly."

The young pilot looked away from his grandmother, his eyes smoldering with some painful memory.

"They made all the hits look like accidents—you know, someone crashes into one of these asteroids in the belt." Casca waved a hand to indicate the complex planetary system quietly shining in miniature in the middle of the room. "Or a couple of patrol ships crash into each other. Or someone's engine fails on reentry and blows up. There are minefields in orbit around both Atterra planets. We *knew* it wasn't accidental, so we stopped flying—we didn't want to lose any more ships, or any more good pilots, when it was obvious we were going to need people who knew how to fly and how to fight. But the second we stopped flying, they came and rounded up most of the fleet."

Casca hesitated, then continued very carefully, "My son, Rendal, was one of a few who made it home to Atterra Bravo after being attacked. He managed to tell us what he'd seen. He'd had an encounter with a pair of TIE fighters. What were two TIE fighters doing in orbit around Atterra Bravo? And why would they have shot down a private law-enforcement starfighter? Rendal made it back alive, and we managed to repair his ship, but he . . ." Casca paused again, swallowed, and finally finished, "It took him a long time to die."

She reached across to touch her grandson lightly on the shoulder; it wasn't obvious if she did it to reassure the boy or to reassure herself. Maybe both.

"I'm sorry," Leia said quietly. "I'm sorry about your son." She turned to Reeve for a moment, and added, "And he was also your father. I'm sorry."

The boy nodded, biting his lip. He turned his face away from her, avoiding having to respond aloud.

"And I'm sorry about Atterra," Leia finished. She gazed at the miniature planets and then asked Casca another pointed question. "Do you know where you are now?"

Casca looked around as if she expected the room might give her a clue. At last she turned back to Leia and said wearily, "No, I don't. I—I don't know *who* you are, either."

Leia nodded in wry agreement. She paced away from the two strangers. "Again, I apologize. My name is Leia Organa."

Casca's eyes flew wide. She obviously knew the name. "You *were* part of the old Rebel Alliance," she said. "And if I'm not mistaken, you *do* have connections in the Senate. Have we come to the right place entirely by accident?"

"Maybe not entirely by accident," said Leia, shaking her head. "As for the place, I can't tell you where you are without having to keep you imprisoned here. And I don't really want to have to do that. But—"

She turned back.

"But I can assure you, if you are who you say you are, you've come to the right place. So if you're willing to cooperate with me—to wait here, perhaps, while I follow up on your story—then maybe I can find a way to help you."

Casca Panzoro and her grandson turned to look at each other once again. This time, they held each other's eyes. For the first time, Rose saw some expression other than fear or pain in their faces.

She saw hope.

The soldier Leia had sent out earlier came back then, carrying a tray with two mugs and a pile of protein portions.

"All right, everybody get back to work. And, Sergeant, find these two travelers someplace where they can eat in peace," Leia ordered. "But keep them strictly under guard. I want to talk to Fossil."

Hammer's crew started to file out after the others. Leia said quickly, "Not you four. I want to talk to you, too."

05

LEIA SURVEYED the bomber crew, her expression giving away nothing.

They all stood at attention. After a moment Leia laughed.

"You are *all so serious.*"

"Only when I'm around," Fossil rumbled ominously.

"You can sit down," Leia told the bomber crew. "I know you're tired. And you still haven't had your routine debriefing. You don't need to oversee the unpacking of the probe droids—we'll turn that over to the intelligence team."

Paige, Rose, and the rest of the crew all looked to Fossil, their commander, for confirmation that they could sit. The Old Lady gave them a slow blink of approval, her crystalline eyes folding shut for a long second.

When they'd taken their seats, Leia came straight to the point.

"How did you pick up your hitchhikers?"

Hammer's pilot, Finch Dallow, acted as spokesman for the crew. He told Leia and Fossil how the two Atterran refugees had come to be aboard the StarFortress as it made the jump to lightspeed.

"Casca Panzoro's story is very convincing," Leia said. "But . . ."

"They could be First Order spies," Fossil acknowledged in her deep, sonorous voice. "I find it most difficult to believe the elaborate tale of how that cobweb of a human boy managed to outfly a patrol of six TIE fighters."

Finch shrugged. "His aerobatics were pretty extraordinary. You don't have to be a beefy hero to fly like a crackerjack."

Privately, Rose agreed with Fossil. Reeve Panzoro seemed much too easy to scare. He'd covered up his fear with rude defiance, but that wasn't the same as mastering it. Rose knew that all too well. Reeve had managed to make a daring escape, but Rose wouldn't want to have to depend on him in a fight.

Paige backed Finch. "Reeve's exactly the pilot I'd have taken with me if I were Casca Panzoro—someone I already knew and trusted. Someone I cared about." She threw Rose a grin. "Family."

"It is a beautiful distraction, their family relationship," Fossil pointed out. "And it may all be part of the perfect ruse—a careful plan for boarding unknown ships and tracing them to the source. You cannot follow or track a ship through lightspeed. But if you place a witness aboard the ship and lull the ship's crew into believing that witness's story . . ."

"It's something we have to consider," Leia agreed. "But I think it's unlikely—they don't know that we are a movement in opposition to the First Order. They think we're a sympathetic military outpost that might help them. And I *feel* they're telling the truth."

"You are always *feeling* things," said Fossil disapprovingly.

Rose was frowning. She didn't realize it until she found Leia looking straight at her, singling her out.

"You feel it, too?" the general asked her mildly.

Rose swallowed. She glanced at Fossil for approval to speak.

"Answer her question," Rose's commander directed.

Rose felt Paige's hand touch her lightly on the arm, quick and reassuring.

"I don't *feel* anything," Rose said. "Not in the way you mean. Not through anything like . . . like the Force. But I think that boy was telling the truth. He was scared." *And a bit sassy,* she added privately in her head. "I could see he was scared when we first met him."

"A good spy would have pulled that off easily," Leia said. "You reported that you were all pointing blasters at him as he got out of his ship."

"He wasn't scared of the blasters," Rose said. "He was scared of the flight he'd just made. He was *relieved* to be out of his ship."

Leia frowned. "What makes you think that?"

"I feel that way all the time after a hop," Rose admitted. Then she added quickly, in her own defense, "I'm better at controlling it."

Paige suddenly agreed. "Rose is right. I saw it, too."

At that moment the sensor at the entrance to the room lit up, and Leia moved to answer the door. Vober Dand came in, the big bearded Tarsunt who was the Resistance base's controller. He'd been on hand when the heavy bomber had landed.

"Here's the report you requested," Vober told the general, handing her a datapad.

Hammer's crew didn't expect Leia to share with them whatever she was reading, and were surprised when she looked up and said frankly, "Well, their ship's no doubt from Atterra Bravo. The electronic log shows it's never been outside the system before—it's equipped for lightspeed but has only ever made short cross-system hops. And there's a corporate imprint saying it was built for the Outside Unit Radicore Elements Mining Company, whatever that is. It's a very old registration but it could well still be valid. They did say they'd stolen the ship."

She passed the datapad to Fossil.

"So far their story remains plausible," Fossil said.

She didn't say anything else, and *Hammer*'s crew waited awkwardly, wondering where their commander and general were going to take this next.

"They wanted supplies," Fossil said. Her glittering platelike eyes were unreadable. "We could provide that."

"How could we provide that?" Vober grumbled.

"We, the heavy bombers of the Cobalt and Crimson Squadrons, could make such a delivery," said Fossil. "We could make a series of runs to their planet and drop what they need in canister rockets carried in our bomb racks. It would be of little difficulty and we could do it quickly."

Fossil turned her gigantic, unreadable crystalline eyes directly on Rose.

"You found your power baffler worked successfully?" she asked.

"Well, it's not the prettiest thing I ever put together," Rose said. "But the little monster did work. I kept worrying that the links would disconnect, but even when we took a couple of direct hits from automatic cannon fire, everything held together."

Paige added spontaneously, "Part of the reason the baffler worked so well is because of the Atterra system itself.

Having all those asteroids to hide behind in the Atterra Belt meant that no one could *see* us a lot of the time. And because we didn't seem to be emitting any power, we were completely hidden right up until we entered each planet's orbit."

"Apart from the direct hits from the automatic cannon we mapped," Nix corrected.

Rose jumped to Paige's defense. "Well, we'll never go *there* again."

General Leia Organa held up one hand, and the bomber crew all immediately stopped arguing.

Leia shook her head. "It sounds like it's a mission we might be able to pull off." She turned to Vober to reassure him. "But I'm not authorizing anything until we've taken a look at some of the data they brought back."

Finally, she turned to Fossil. "This crew's all yours now," she said. "You can take over with your usual operational debriefing. But I'd like to listen in if it's all right with you."

———

Leia didn't say a single word while Fossil questioned the bomber crew about the details of their recent mission. She waited until the debriefing was over. Then, as the crew began to leave, she walked across to Paige and laid one friendly hand on her shoulder.

"The Atterra crisis must really make you think of home," she said.

Paige nodded. She was still seated, and with Leia's hand resting on her shoulder, it would have been awkward for Paige to stand up. Rose didn't get up, either, waiting for her sister.

"I know just how that feels," Leia said. "I think of Alderaan every time I hear a story like this. I think of home, and all these years later, I *still* think of Alderaan as home. When I hear a story like yours, or like Reeve and Casca's, in a flash I think, *If we win this time, I'll be able to go back*—and an instant later I remember it's gone. We *can't* let it keep happening."

She paused.

"I want to help them," she said. "And Casca's right: if we *don't* help now, the First Order will grow bolder and do it again and again. And then it will be too late to avoid war. But my own Resistance movement isn't large enough to act as a galactic security force, and I can't just rush into a rescue mission. We need a plan."

Leia put a hand on Rose's shoulder, too, so that the general was standing between the Tico sisters and including them both in her request.

"I'd like to send you to Atterra Bravo as advance scouts," Leia said. "I'd like to get a couple of real live people on the ground there to confirm Casca Panzoro's story. If what she tells us is true, I'll also need someone on the ground to establish a link with the Bravo Rising organizers before we begin smuggling in the supplies they need so desperately."

"An intelligence mission?" Paige asked with interest.

Leia shook her head. "Scouting, not spying. *Reconnaissance*. Think it over. Talk about it together. If you don't want to do it yourselves, I can ask someone more experienced in this line of work. But it's a mission that you've a right to, so I'm offering it to you first."

Leia lifted her hands, freeing Rose and Paige so they could go.

"Take twenty-four hours," Leia said. "With people already dying of thirst there, this will have to be a quick decision. But it'll take us a day to equip an appropriate ship. So you've got a day. Think about it. Talk it over. Get back to me tomorrow."

————

Rose thought about it all the rest of that day—all through the report she had to make in the technicians' assembly about the success of the baffler, and all through the hours she then spent checking the baffler's plugs while below her the StarFortress crew chief, Hadeen Bissel, directed a repair team as they removed the bomb clip that had been damaged when the Atterran ship had made its awkward crash landing.

Rose *thought* about it, and there was no doubt in her mind that she wanted to do it.

But she and Paige hadn't *talked* about it yet.

They'd scarcely had a moment together since their return to D'Qar. When they'd finally been able to collapse in their shared bunk block that night, Rose had fallen asleep instantly, completely exhausted as she always was after a hop.

Paige woke her early the next morning. "Come on," she said to Rose. "Let's go look at the forest."

The wilderness of D'Qar, just after sunrise, was a place of unsettling loveliness. You couldn't walk far into the unspoiled forest; the only trails were those made by Resistance hunters and foragers. Paige was always hoping for a glimpse of wildlife in this lush jungle, though she and Rose had never encountered anything other than birds and insects.

Some of these were big enough—or small enough, in the case of the swarms of stinging midges—to make Rose wary. There had been no animal life at all on her icebound, twilit planet home of Hays Minor, so far from the sun that all foodstuffs had to be grown under artificial light.

Two sonar swallows, no bigger than Rose's hand and iridescent as an oil slick, swooped down and sat on Paige's shoulder. These little birds, which always traveled in pairs or flocks, seemed to find noise of any kind irresistible and were fascinated by human speech.

"I love it here," said Paige. "You know what I'd like to do? Come out here every day and just study all of D'Qar's birds. Take holos and record their songs and the way they fly, and make a catalogue that lists them all."

The birds on D'Qar were the first real animals the Tico sisters had ever seen.

Back home, when they were younger and before their world had been devastated, Paige had been obsessed with animals. Her enthusiasm had infected her younger sister, too. Though Hays Minor had been too cold to support native wildlife on its surface, the walls of the Tico family pod had been vibrant with images of steeds and wildcats and herds of livestock and giant sea bulls. All the games Paige had made up as a child had involved taking care of animals, or riding them, or healing them. And Rose had followed along, as she always did.

"Seems like the only birds we ever get to count are the spy droid variety," Rose grumbled. "Why are you so absolutely optimistic *all the time*?"

Paige laid her arm along Rose's shoulders and leaned over to hum in her ear. The two sonar swallows hopped along Paige's arm, following the sound of her voice, until they had hopped onto Rose's shoulder. When Paige backed away, the beautiful glimmering creatures were fluttering their tinkling feathers by the side of Rose's head.

"I do it to keep your spirits up, of course," said Paige. "I promised Dad I'd look after you."

Paige touched the pale gold medallion around her neck.

"We always said we were going to travel the galaxy together, and we're doing it, right?"

Rose nearly responded with natural sarcasm: *Yeah, we're on a luxury cruise.*

But Paige was serious and joyful, and it seemed mean to shoot her down. They'd both wanted it so badly while they were growing up in the cold and the dark—to walk in the sun together on some green-and-blue planet warmed by a bright star.

Rose let Paige have the last word this time.

"We're doing it," Rose repeated slowly, aware that Paige didn't just mean D'Qar. "So what do you think? You've thought about it, haven't you?"

"Thought about what?" Paige said.

"Oh, nuts and bolts," Rose exclaimed. "What do you think I mean, opening an interplanetary zoo? Selling Haysian jewelry to rich senators? About Leia's mission, of course! About going spying on Atterra Bravo!"

"*Reconnaissance,*" Paige said. "Not spying. Not intelligence work—just cross-checking information."

"Well? She told us to think about it. Have you thought about it?"

"Someone needs to do it," Paige said. "But I'm not sure it should be us."

Rose frowned at her sister in the cool half light of the sunrise and asteroid shadow.

"Why not?"

"I don't want anything to happen to you. I'm *responsible* for you."

"We're pretty much up to our ears in it together already," Rose pointed out.

"I always get second thoughts when I'm out here in the early morning," Paige admitted. "It's so peaceful. And it makes me long for an ordinary life."

"*Peaceful* isn't really in the Resistance heavy bomber job description," Rose said.

"Of course not. It's what we're working on," Paige answered.

They walked a little farther along the trail.

"Have *you* thought about it?" Paige asked suddenly.

"Of course I've thought about it!"

"And?"

"I'm ready to leave after breakfast!"

Paige laughed.

"The thing is," Rose said, "I wouldn't do it alone. You might do it without me, but I wouldn't do it without you. I'm not scared of ending up dead—I'd be just as dead if the TIE fighters had blown us up yesterday." She used the babyish nickname she'd called her older sister when they were very little. "But Pae-Pae . . ." Rose gulped in a breath. "I'm scared of us not being a team anymore."

"You're so *cute.*" Paige laughed.

Rose rolled her eyes. "Don't be embarrassing!"

"I'm your big sister," Paige said. "That's my job. That, and keeping you alive."

"Why do you think Leia asked *us?*" Rose wondered. "She said it was our *right.* Why would we get the first shot at this mission?"

"Well, there's the obvious—we've proved we're versatile," Paige answered. "I'm a crack shot with a laser cannon, and I'm a reasonable pilot; you've become an expert at tinkering with quirky hyperdrives and auxiliary fuel systems."

Rose snorted. The sound was lost in the sudden drone of a small swarm of tiny golden dragonflies that whizzed past their heads. Rose ducked, and Paige laughed again.

"You were the first person Leia came to when she wanted that power baffler for the last hop," Paige said. "And we've been to Atterra already, so we know what to expect when we go back. But also . . . I think Leia's *counting* on us wanting to do it together. She knows we're a team."

"Well, then! We have to go together so you can keep me alive," Rose said. "So let's get ready for our unexpected spy mission."

"Reconnaissance," Paige insisted. "Stop calling it a spy mission."

Then she added, "You know we won't actually be alone. The pilot will go with us."

"What pilot?"

"The Atterran pilot. Reeve Panzoro."

"Oh, you are *kidding me.* Please tell me you are kidding me."

"One of those Atterrans will have to stay here, as a sort of goodwill hostage, but we're going to need a guide. A contact on the ground. Casca Panzoro wanted to go herself and leave her grandson here where he's safe, but *we'll* be safer with a good local pilot along in that rock storm of the Atterra Belt. And if anything goes wrong, Casca seems to be a more valuable hostage for the Resistance . . . or a more useful ally."

Rose let her doubts about Reeve Panzoro come to the surface.

"Okay, I get that he's a fabulous pilot, and I get why Casca would want to take him with her when she got *out* of Atterra. But do you trust him? And is Leia really going to make one of them stay here while the other goes back with a couple of strangers? Can you imagine if she did that to *us*?"

"You know she wouldn't," said Paige. "Not if we didn't agree to it. So it must be okay with them."

"You just said Casca was a potential hostage. I bet they didn't get a choice."

Paige looked uncomfortable. "Well, maybe they didn't. But it's a different situation than ours."

Rose sighed. "Just great," she grumbled. "A spy mission with someone who might not want to be there. We don't have any idea if we can trust him. And he's just so—" She struggled for the right word.

"Young?" Paige suggested.

"Scared," Rose said.

"Well, so are you. You said you're scared all the time. You said it's part of you, like wearing your Otomok medallion."

"Yes, but . . ." Rose didn't really want to admit how much Reeve's fearfulness scared *her*. She hoped her own fears were never so obvious to other people. "That's just worrying about *myself*. Now I'm going to have to be responsible for *someone else*. I see what you mean about not wanting to go because you don't want anything to happen to me—I don't want anything terrible to happen to Reeve Panzoro and I don't even know him!"

Paige laughed. "That's just what it feels like to be a big sister," she said affectionately. "It doesn't stop me."

"Well, it's not going to stop me, either," said Rose with determination.

06

SCARCELY A DAY later, Paige, Rose, and Reeve were back in the Atterra system.

Once all the preparations had been taken care of, the flight had been straightforward, thanks to a new version of Rose's power baffler. They'd made it through the belt and the blockade and the minefield, and now they were skimming along the surface of an ominously yellow briny ocean on Atterra Bravo.

Rose had been restless during the lightspeed jump. The cabin of the ship they were traveling in was too cramped for her to get comfortable enough to sleep. And she'd been worrying, worrying, worrying about whether her half-baked equipment was going to work. If any of it didn't, they were all probably dead.

Once they'd entered the Atterra system, they'd had to change course four times on their way in to Atterra Bravo to avoid a handful of lone hunters and one patrol.

Now they'd made it to the planet's surface undetected.

But looking at the turbulent yellow sea that stretched end-lessly away from them on all sides, and seeing no obvious place to land, Rose wondered if they weren't all going to end up dead anyway.

Paige was trying to be patient.

"Would it help," she asked Reeve Panzoro in her calm-est of calm voices, "if we flew back out into orbit and then reentered Bravo's atmosphere from different coordinates? Maybe you'd recognize where we're going from higher up."

"Maybe . . ." Reeve answered uncertainly. "But I don't think going back out will help. I don't know any other coordinates. I'm not a human compass . . . I used the coor-dinates Ms. Casca told me to."

"Well, they're not working, so we need a plan B," Rose said.

"What do you think, then, Rose?" Paige prompted.

Rose was trying hard not to panic. She hated being lost; she hated having to trust Reeve to find the way; and above all she hated the feeling that it would be her fault if anything happened to him. She hated not knowing what to do.

The ship's a known factor, Rose reminded herself. *What's best for the ship?*

"The human compass is right," Rose said grudgingly. "Going back into orbit isn't going to do us any good. The extra power to get us out of the planet's atmosphere will be too strong for the baffler to hide. It's risky enough that we have to do it when we leave. If we do it more than once, someone'll notice."

"I said I *wasn't* a human compass," Reeve grumbled.

Paige's shoulders rose and fell. She didn't sigh aloud, but Rose knew it was a sigh.

"Can you guys put a little less energy into your snappy comebacks and a bit more into figuring out where we are?" Paige requested, scanning the horizon for someplace to land.

"All my energy is going into keeping this ship from going down," Rose said.

The *Little Vixen* was a very small, very battered civilian private transport they had been assigned for this mission, and it was a prized possession for the Resistance. The *Vixen* wasn't big enough to carry any kind of freight. It was an outdated model of a ship that had never been popular. It didn't appear to be armed (though it was, very lightly, with a single small laser cannon operated by the pilot); its realspace cruise speed was so slow it couldn't outfly a landspeeder. It was so shabby and ordinary that it was very easily overlooked.

It was perfect for reconnaissance.

It could land anywhere. It had been fitted with a sophisticated Class 1 hyperdrive so that it traveled through hyperspace at the same rate as an X-wing. It also carried a tracking device that allowed the Resistance to monitor its movements when it reached an agreed-on destination. This was programmed to purge its files and self-destruct if anyone tried to interfere with it while it was operating. Essentially, if the ship were intercepted by an enemy, it would become a suicide device.

In addition to these peculiarities, Rose had fitted the unassuming vehicle with another power baffler, a miniature version of the one she'd fixed up in *Hammer*. It took up the same amount of space as a passenger and a half, which reduced the available room considerably in an already cramped cabin that wasn't actually designed for long-distance galactic travel.

Under the circumstances, an uncomfortable journey was the least of their worries.

The Atterran boy hadn't had any trouble familiarizing himself with the *Little Vixen*'s flight characteristics. Rose had to admit he was a born pilot. All he'd needed was a few pointers from Paige and he was in control. He knew very little about setting the complex coordinates for hyperspace, and for security Paige hadn't let him see where they were starting from anyway, but in the realspace of the Atterra system he was a secure and confident navigator. He'd known what he was doing when he'd guided them down to the surface of his home planet.

He hadn't gotten lost until they entered the atmosphere of Atterra Bravo.

Now it seemed he didn't have any idea where he was. He flew hesitantly, zigzagging over churning, steaming seas. It was obvious that he was growing more and more nervous.

Paige asked next, "Can we do a float landing on this ocean and power down while we get our bearings?"

"Don't even think about it," Rose warned. "The ship's telling me the sea's too acidic to tolerate. Five minutes sitting on the surface will start to eat away its hull."

"Well, we've got ourselves flying in circles," Paige said. "We can't go on forever."

"I used the right coordinates," Reeve said stubbornly. "This is where Ms. Casca told me to reenter the atmosphere for Firestone." He added resentfully, *"Maybe if you'd let her come along . . ."*

Sympathy and irritation warred inside Rose. She knew how he felt about being separated from his grandmother.

"We weren't given that option," Paige reminded him. "Now I'm beat, and so are you. Haven't you had enough already? Rose isn't rated to fly this thing, and we can't wander around down here on autopilot waiting for a blockade patrol to catch up with us. We're going to have to land and get some sleep for a few hours. Find me an island that's not poisonous or covered with acidic quicksand."

"He's not a human compass," Rose pointed out helpfully.

Reeve didn't answer. His eyes went narrow and angry, but he held his temper as he scanned the horizon. "I *know* where I am. I'm just not sure how to get home from here. The sea only boils north of the Firestone Islands, so we can't be far." He held his course. "Try that way."

Paige and Rose stared with tired eyes in the direction Reeve was pointing.

A stubborn, worn volcanic cone broke the horizon, blue in the distance over a sea that now gleamed golden in the low sunlight. The mountain grew quickly—it was nearer than Rose had at first thought. Reeve powered back as the *Little Vixen* approached the land.

The island couldn't have been more than a kilometer wide and a couple of kilometers long. There were no beaches: it was a low mountainous outcrop whose glassy deep-blue slopes plunged directly into the acidic sea, which ate away at them until they became cliffs.

Paige took a quick reading of the terrain. "There." She pointed. "You see it?"

"The second shelf? The one with the ledge like a bowl?"

"It won't give us much cover, but it's flat."

"Paige," Rose began, "maybe for the landing you should take over from the human—"

"I can land," said the boy fiercely.

"He's okay," Paige said.

He was, too. He was sulky, angry, defensive, lost, and scared, but he knew how to fly. As he was touching down the unfamiliar ship, featherlight on the narrow ledge, Paige murmured close to Rose's ear, "Actually, he's a better pilot than I am."

"He's too nervous, though," Rose muttered back. "He's scaring *me*."

Paige didn't answer, which made Rose think that Reeve must be scaring her a little, too.

They were all utterly exhausted. They erected a pop-up shelter so that Paige and Reeve, the pilots, would be able to lie down.

But Rose didn't get the luxury of sleep. She stood on guard, watching the sky. It was the only way Paige could relax enough to get the rest she so desperately needed— knowing Rose would wake her if something happened.

This was definitely not what Rose and Paige had meant when they'd made their childhood pact to travel the galaxy together.

All the same, Rose couldn't help feeling a little twist of excitement and anticipation as she breathed in this new, sharp, faintly rotten-egg air and watched Atterra's countless asteroids grow brighter, too far away to be moons but bigger than stars. The sun set and a purple twilight began to fall.

Rose always felt a small, guilty pleasure in any mission that took her to a new and unknown world.

She fingered the pale gold medallion that had swung loose from where it was tucked into her collar. They were all wearing plain civilian work clothes, something that might blend in if they were seen. Rose's medallion was engraved with the planetary system of Otomok, and Rose knew it would raise dangerous questions if she were caught by anyone. But she needed to keep it near her—a connection to her lost home, a reminder of the cause she was fighting for, and a physical link, always, to her big sister.

She tucked the pendant back beneath her undertunic, where it lay safe against her skin. Rose looked again at the sky.

It was absolutely the most beautiful sky she'd ever seen. It was even better from the planet's surface than from space. The asteroids, beginning to glow as the sun sank lower, looked like tiny hanging lamps against pale blue silk.

Then Rose noticed one of them growing brighter much faster than the others.

At first she thought it was a meteor.

But she wasn't fooled for longer than a second.

It was a ship, and it was heading straight for them.

"Get up! Get up!" Rose started tearing down the pop-up shelter even before she'd evicted its sleeping inhabitants. *"Paige! Paige! Reeve!* Wake up—we've got to move!"

Paige was awake instantly. She leaped past Rose, threw herself into the *Vixen*'s cockpit, and started powering up. Rose had to reach into the shelter to haul the still half-asleep Reeve out by his armpits so she could fully collapse the tent.

"Hey," he protested blearily, "what do you think you're doing?"

Rose threw the thinfoil pop-up package into the ship, considered giving Reeve a kick, and decided it wouldn't help. She grabbed him by the arm again and bellowed in his ear, *"We've been seen!"*

She wasn't sure that was true yet, but it certainly would be in another minute or so. *"Get back in the ship."*

He scrambled, half crawling, up the small boarding ramp. Rose tumbled over him, slamming the hatch shut behind her. Paige took off before Rose had managed to pick herself up.

Reeve was suddenly wide-awake and crouching over Paige's shoulder, shouting panicked directions at her.

"No, no, no, don't head north! There's nothing out there till you get to Rockland Plate! The Firestones are in the other—"

"We'll head back when we lose the guy behind us!" Paige snarled, losing her cool for once. "Spinning rockets, this thing is *so slow.* Rose, help me out here!"

"How?" Rose cried.

"I don't know! Can't the power baffler hide us some-how?"

"It only disguises the power output. As long as they can see us, we can't hide. Maybe when it's dark— It's *nearly* dark!" She looked east. "Head for the dark!"

"But we're *so. Totally. Slow.* If they've got a search beam, we'll never shake them."

Reeve pointed over Paige's shoulder. He and Rose cried in unison, "Keep going east!"

"I don't believe it," Paige gasped. "You're both human compasses."

"Ha ha ha." Rose crouched anxiously at the rear port-hole, watching the bright light that was the other ship grow steadily, speedily closer.

Maybe it's friendly, she thought desperately. *Maybe it's one of those security ships Casca Panzoro was talking about. . . .*

When she saw the searchlight beam probing out toward her, she knew in her bones that it wasn't anyone friendly.

If they were caught in the beam they wouldn't even be able to hide in the dark.

"*Climb,*" Rose cried. "*Climb!* Forget east. Get out of their path!"

The boy suddenly leaped into life. "*But wait till they get close!*"

His voice was unsteady, but his brain was obviously

working. Rose remembered that he'd managed to outfly a squadron of TIE fighters. He was good at escaping.

"If you slow down just when they think they've got us, it might take them by surprise," Reeve gasped. "Then they'll overtake us and have to double back. Head straight up while they're turning."

"Kid's better at flying than he is at directions," Rose said grimly, and Paige answered just as grimly, "Shut up. Tell me when they get close."

Rose crouched, staring out the rear porthole, watching the other ship gain on them second by second.

She winced, momentarily blinded, when the search beam caught them.

Now the *Little Vixen* was illuminated like a dragonfly with sun on its wings.

It was only seconds before the first blast of laser fire sizzled the air directly over their heads. They all cringed.

"Hold on—*hold on!*" Rose yelled. "It was just a warning. They'd have hit us if they'd meant it. They can see us perfectly. . . ."

She couldn't see *them* perfectly—the searchlight beam was blinding her. All she could tell was that their attacker was a lot bigger than they were.

"They want to make us follow them, or tow us home as pets, or something. They'll be right behind us in just a couple of seconds. Get ready to climb. . . ."

Rose forced herself to wait patiently for the exact right moment.

"Three . . . two . . ."

It felt like the longest countdown of her life.

"ONE! Hit the sky!"

Paige set the vertical thrust to full power, and the *Little Vixen* rocketed skyward out of the beam of light.

Rose screamed, "Keep going! Keep going! They're still looping back. . . ."

The light of the *Vixen*'s engines would be visible to their pursuer from below.

"Don't stop climbing till I tell you to!" Rose cried. If they could just get enough height before the searchlight beam caught them again—

The attack ship's beams swept around in a tight circle and then pointed skyward as it, too, began to climb, much faster than the small Resistance reconnaissance ship.

"Lights out," Rose said, and Paige and Reeve switched everything off.

The patrol ship soared past them in the sky without seeing them. Their pursuer obviously thought they were climbing away into space a lot faster than they were capable of climbing.

"YES!" they cheered together.

"Now we just glide away into the dark," Paige said, her

voice shaking, but with something of its usual calm command back in it.

"Wow," Rose breathed, giddy with the success of the trick. "Hey, we all worked together pretty well there! Sorry I shouted at you, Paige." She choked back a laugh. "That's the first time you've *ever* let me boss you around like that."

"South," Reeve yelled wildly. "Head south."

The pursuing ship was circling above them with its searchlight on, hunting for them in the wrong place.

It looked like their desperate bid for freedom was going to work.

Paige had taken the *Vixen* high enough that they were going to be able to glide for several kilometers with their engines idling. When they had to start up the power again, the baffler would mask the low emission it would take to keep going. And now it was dark enough that they couldn't be seen unless the terrible searchlight caught them by accident.

"What do you think, Paige?" Rose panted. "Is it safe to get back on course yet?"

"I don't see any sign of them. . . ."

"South," insisted Reeve.

Paige swung the *Little Vixen* around and headed south.

———

He was right, in the end.

After another hour of flying, without encountering any more patrol ships, they found the outlying uninhabited islets of the Firestone Islands.

Paige let Reeve take over for the landing in the dark; he was obviously at home in this inhospitable terrain.

And this time, they managed to get some sleep.

Within two hours of waking the next morning, they had located the main island of the Firestone archipelago.

They were all nervous about flying in daylight now. It was likely that the ship that had spotted them the night before would come back to try to track them down. Their little Resistance reconnaissance ship was still operating under the cover of Rose's power baffler, but of course that wasn't going to stop them from being seen in broad daylight.

But Reeve was excited as well as nervous. He was home. It was kind of painful to watch; Rose could see how much he loved this barren place.

"See the pipelines down there?" Reeve pointed sweepingly. "That's where the big hydro farms begin. Keep going! We can land in the pumice forest. It's not far now. Ms. Casca says no off-worlders ever go there, and from there you can hike along the beach to the Big Settlement. The rock formations give you good cover. I can guide you."

"Sure you can," said Rose drily.

But they did what Reeve suggested.

When they touched down and climbed out of the *Little Vixen*, they were clearly in a different kind of landscape from the one where they'd set down the night before.

Here the ground was no longer glassy, but porous. The towering columns of pumice were worn flat at the tide line where the acidic seas had ebbed and flowed. It was an eerie place, and the fluting of the wind as it whistled through the holes in the pumice stone and between the columns didn't help. It sounded like the air was full of ghosts.

But it wasn't bad walking. Paige and Rose carried blasters, just in case, in addition to their light packs. They had hidden the ship under a camouflage sheet that blended in with its surroundings. So far the hydro pipelines were the only evidence they'd seen of intelligent life on this barren, bright, and hostile world.

Reeve was eager and anxious all at the same time. "It'll take us a few hours to walk to the settlement. Atterra Bravo's a safe place for walking—there isn't any native wildlife here."

"No native wildlife!" Rose echoed. "There goes our safari! So the only thing we have to worry about is the First Order invaders?"

Reeve was instantly sober. "Well, yes. They've taken over the hydro farms, and they have a lot of ships here. There's a trickle of water still allowed to the administrators, like Ms. Casca, so they have someone on site who knows the farms."

Reeve paused.

"We've tried to share the water," he added in a low voice. "A lot of people have their own condensers. But—but most of the settlement died of thirst in the first two weeks of the blockade."

He turned his face away abruptly, as he often did when emotion hit him hard.

After a quiet moment, Paige said, "I'm sorry."

After another pause, Rose added, "And me. I'm sorry, too."

It wasn't exactly what had happened back in Otomok, Paige and Rose's home star system. The destruction there had happened differently. But the end result had been the same.

"Let's get going," said Paige.

"Yeah, let's get going," Rose repeated gruffly. "Let's get this safari over with."

They started walking along the harsh, porous beach.

They marched without speaking for the first half hour or so. There was no sound but the acidic waves, which were too dangerous to get close to. After about five kilometers they came to a small curving bay, so sheltered from the wind that the surface of the sea lay flat and still.

They stopped there, out of the wind, and paused to take careful sips of their water supply. Warned about the peculiarities of the Firestone Islands, they'd come from D'Qar with a portable condenser, but they still had to be sparing with their water. As they stood looking over the ominous beauty of the golden bay, Reeve fretted, "I wonder if we should have flown straight to the Big Settlement. It's dangerous flying in daylight, but it would be faster. Ms. Casca would have had a better plan than me. . . ."

"You need to start thinking for yourself," Rose advised him. "You're the safari guide, not Ms. Casca!"

Reeve's face clouded. "Well, what's wrong with relying on someone who knows better than you? You do the same thing."

"Since when?" Rose challenged.

"Do you even hear yourself? *'Yeah, let's get going.' 'Me too, Big Sister.'* You don't do *anything* without making sure it's okay with Paige. You even apologized for telling her how to hide from that First Order ship last night!"

Paige laughed. "That's true, you did."

"I only apologized for yelling at you!" Rose started to protest.

It wasn't true that she needed Paige's say-so to get things done. Rose had her own skills, her own accomplishments, her own projects and assignments. People *trusted* her. *Leia* trusted her. Rose had invented the power baffler herself, and she was in charge of the tracking equipment that told the Resistance back on D'Qar that they'd landed safely three times since they arrived on Atterra Bravo.

But it *was* true that Rose hadn't wanted to take responsibility for Reeve.

"We're on this hop together because we're *sisters*," Rose said defensively. "Not because I can't do anything without Paige! We work well together—"

She stopped suddenly. *He's just a kid,* Rose reminded herself. *A scared kid puffing himself up at the expense of someone he's sure isn't going to hurt him. And he can't stop thinking about his grandmother, who's been left behind in another star system.*

With a huge effort, Rose reined herself in. She turned quickly to Paige with a different question. "How long can we stay on this planet?"

"We can stay here three days, if we're going to be self-sufficient," Paige answered.

"So," said Rose.

"We'll be fine," said Paige. "The air's cool and the walking's easy. So let's enjoy the safari!"

Rose gave her older sister a dirty look. But she didn't answer. She screwed the lid back on her water flask.

Then Reeve hissed suddenly, "Get back behind the stone columns—*fast.*"

07

IT WAS the first time Rose had ever heard Reeve Panzoro say anything that sounded like a command rather than a protest.

She swung around to look at him. He grabbed her by the elbow. The jolt made Rose let go of her flask. Before she could pick it up, Reeve was dragging her away from the beach, toward the shelter of the rock formations.

"Hey, wait—"

"Just get under cover."

With his other hand, he gave Paige a push, as well.

In Reeve's voice there was something so urgent, and so terrified, that neither one of the Tico sisters argued with him. All three of them ran for the protective camouflage of the volcanic columns.

When they'd nearly reached the tall rock formations, the terrain underfoot becoming more uneven, Rose looked back over her shoulder.

There was another ship approaching the beach. Rose

couldn't be sure, but it didn't look to her like the one that had been chasing them the night before. This one seemed a lot bigger. It was skimming low along the surface of the yellow sea but not close enough to damage its hull, just the way Paige and Reeve had been flying when they'd first arrived on Atterra Bravo. But it rode closer to the surface than Paige and Reeve had, because the water of the sheltered bay was so still.

It was an enormous ship. It wasn't a privately owned launch or even a police cruiser. It was a big freighter or a transport of some kind. There wasn't room for it to set down on the beach, but it hovered closer and closer over the bay, almost as if it were about to land there.

"Get back—we're dead if someone sees us," panted Reeve. They were among the towering pumice formations, but the columns weren't close enough or wide enough to hide them completely.

"We'd better stop moving," Reeve said suddenly in a low voice.

The three of them crouched low, wedged tightly into a cluster of treelike tilted rocks that leaned against each other at the top, forming a sort of cave. Paige knelt and, leaning with her elbows against a stone, focused on the approaching ship through her macrobinoculars.

"What is it?" Rose asked.

"Death transport," the young Atterran pilot gasped. "They do sweeps to gather people up—"

The ship's repulsorlifts grew louder as it crept dangerously near to the surface of the acidic bay.

Rose raised her own macrobinoculars to her eyes to get a better look, fascinated and horrified as a wide, ramp-like hatch yawned open on the hovering transport. Rose could see half a dozen First Order stormtroopers, wearing the menacing white armor that was so similar to that of the former Imperial stormtroopers. They struggled with crates and pulleys and other equipment at the entrance to the transport.

"What are they doing here?" she whispered to Reeve. "You said off-worlders stay away from this part of the planet. And what did you mean—*death transport?*"

"I said the pumice forest was safe," Reeve answered distractedly. "I didn't mean—I meant our *world* is safe. I mean, it used to be safe. This—this transport is full of dead prisoners. They gather people up and fly them into orbit, but their holding cells aren't atmospherically controlled, so the prisoners die in space. Then they dump them off in our oceans—"

Reeve swallowed before he continued.

"It's an easy way to dispose of bodies. They've got a couple of big transports they keep on Atterra Alpha, and they bring them over here and round people up. It's the perfect place to get rid of the evidence . . . the acid sea doesn't leave much behind."

Rose wondered if he'd seen this happen before.

Then she wondered *how many times* he'd seen it happen.

Reeve gulped again. He was no longer watching. He whispered, "Ms. Casca thinks—"

Reeve coughed, and corrected himself.

"We think they might be bringing prisoner transports here from other systems, too. It's just so easy to get rid of people here, and then there's no trace of what's happened to them."

Even through her macrobinoculars Rose couldn't tell what was being tipped out of the massive container that had shunted forward through the hatch of the transport. The angle was wrong. And she didn't really want to confirm Reeve's story with her own eyes anyway.

But it seemed pretty obvious that he wasn't making it up.

Reeve was crouched with his face turned aside. "They haven't used this part of Firestone before," he said. "They don't always land in the same spot."

Paige answered quietly, "Let's hope they haven't raided your settlement."

It wasn't the large-scale destruction of a city or a planet. But it was murder all the same.

Sick at heart, Rose didn't want to watch the ship anymore.

But just as she started to lower her macrobinoculars, her eyes were drawn from the transport to the beach. She'd spotted a small thing that stood out against the porous rock.

It was her water flask.

Rose's mouth felt dry just looking at it. She swallowed. Silently, she cursed Reeve for making her drop the flask in the first place, and then she cursed herself for failing to pick it up right away. If anyone on the transport noticed it . . .

Rose gazed through the macrobinoculars again. No one was looking toward the shore; the stormtroopers closest to the end of the ramp were hosing down the now-empty container. They wore thick, lightweight armor that seemed to be treated with some kind of protective coating to withstand splashes from Atterra Bravo's acidic sea.

Suddenly, Rose saw Reeve, appearing much closer through the telescopic lenses than he actually was, darting forward across the open beach.

For twenty seconds, he was completely vulnerable, moving in plain sight out in the open in front of the First Order death transport.

He ran hunkered down, bent low, as near to the ground as he could get without crawling.

"What is he doing?" Paige gasped.

Reeve grabbed Rose's water flask. He looked up quickly through his own macrobinoculars toward the hovering transport, checking to make sure no one had noticed him.

No one had. They were still working on cleaning out the container.

Reeve crept backward toward where Paige and Rose were still hidden.

He went more carefully now than he had when he'd so quickly darted forward. He stared through the macrobinoculars as he moved, keeping his eyes on the transport.

Rose held her breath.

"Made it," Reeve panted, slipping back into the protective shadow of the rock formations. He held out Rose's flask to her.

"You should have waited!" she hissed. "They're nearly done—they'll leave in a minute!"

"It was a time bomb lying there. When they've finished, they always make a low pass to patrol the area in case someone's seen them. They'd have spotted it for sure, and then they'd have dropped someone out to do a search. Especially after that chase in the dark last night, they're bound to make the connection."

"But if they'd seen you *now*?"

"They'd have just got *me*." He drew in a ragged breath. "You two might have been all right."

Paige stared at him, frowning.

Reeve was good at running away, but Rose could hardly believe he'd jumped forward into danger like that. It seemed completely out of character to her. She spoke aloud what she knew her sister was thinking. "You're either very, very brave, or very, very stupid."

Reeve shrugged. "I know I'm not brave, but I'm not stupid, either. It was just what I had to do, right? It was my fault in the first place, and I knew the risks and you didn't. So there wasn't really any choice."

The wide hatch on the transport ship began to close up.

"*Shhh*," Reeve warned. "Sit close against the rocks and don't move. They're going to do their scan of the landscape now."

The whole procedure had taken less than an hour. Less than an hour to get rid of the bodies of a few thousand people and completely wipe any trace of them from the face of the planet. With its doors closed, the transport rumbled slowly up and down the beach. Reeve had been right about them sweeping the area.

By the time the ship had roared away into the sky, Paige and Rose and their guide were all thirsty again, as well as stiff and sore from having to crouch for so long among the rough and uneven rock columns.

After a moment's hesitation, Rose passed her canteen to Reeve.

He had his own canteen, of course. But this shared

drink was a tribute. It was a tribute to what his world had suffered and was suffering—and to the danger he'd risked to save Rose and Paige a few minutes before.

Reeve drank briefly—ceremoniously. He understood.

Then he handed the canteen back to Rose and stood up.

"Well, come on," he said. "What about our safari?"

They made it to Reeve Panzoro's settlement without encountering another ship, though they did see an assortment of craft crossing the sky while they walked. They traveled close to the pumice columns in case they needed to take cover again.

The outer living quarters of the Big Settlement stood empty. The first sign of habitation that the Tico sisters saw in the Firestone Islands was a collection of domed, glittering white saltstone huts with no one inside. Broken doors hung open, swinging gently in the sea wind, and empty water condensers trailed wires in the walled yards around the empty houses. The Big Settlement of Firestone Main Island had become a ghost town.

"There are never any bodies," said Reeve. "When people die, we send them out to sea. It's clean. It's what we've always done."

He choked.

"But we don't—we don't *murder them first*."

"Don't worry. We get you," Rose told him.

There was an inner circle to the compound that was surrounded by a makeshift barricade. It was there that Reeve led Paige and Rose. The way behind the barricade was through a complicated system of tunnels beginning in one of the abandoned houses.

The three of them were greeted, as they emerged, with deep suspicion—by half a dozen gaunt and exhausted-looking people holding an assortment of deadly-looking weapons.

Before anyone could challenge them, one of the Atterran fighters cried out, "Hold fire! It's Reeve! It's *Reeve Panzoro!*"

A man and a woman not much older than Reeve rushed forward to hug him. Another, older man kept a solar crossbow ready to fire; three other seasoned-looking settlers held electric staffs that could clearly do some damage in a fight. There was no reason yet for these people to put their trust in Rose and Paige.

"It's all right—it's all right," Reeve promised. "They're with me."

"Where's Casca?" asked the man with the crossbow.

"She's safe. We made it out. I'll tell you in a minute— she sent me with these . . ."

He hesitated, struggling to come up with the right word, and Rose resisted a wild urge to put in, *Pirates!*

"Emissaries," Reeve came up with triumphantly. He gestured toward Paige and Rose, with a glance into their faces. "These are Paige Tico, pilot, and Rose Tico, flight engineer, representatives of General Leia Organa. General Organa has connections with the New Republic Senate."

He turned to Rose and Paige, with a sweep of his arm to indicate the local settlers. "And this is the Bravo Rising resistance team of Atterra Bravo. My uncle Orion Chalk. The foreman of the Big Settlement hydro farm before it was taken away from us, Darrus Rantarovo. And this is the chief instructor from the Firestone Technical Academy, Tanya Helios."

The chief instructor of the Technical Academy stepped forward. She held out her hand to Paige, and then to Rose. "Thank you. Thank you for being here." Darrus, following Tanya, shook their hands, as well, but didn't say anything. He seemed too choked up to speak.

Paige and Rose gave each other sideways glances. After what they'd seen that day, there wasn't any doubt in their minds. They knew they would do whatever they could to help these people.

08

PAIGE WAS WORRIED about the Big Settlement's desperate lack of water. She didn't want to have to count on the Firestone Islands to provide for her or Rose when the Atterrans clearly could barely manage to provide for themselves. So she agreed to stay with them one day only, and they had to make plans right away for how the Resistance could help them.

The assembly was Reeve Panzoro's idea.

Bravo Rising called a group meeting in a covered market area in the center of the settlement. They held it in the evening to allow time to send messengers several kilometers across the landscape on pedal-powered veloflyers. There was next to no fuel for generating power in the Firestone Islands anymore. All the solar and wind power went toward condensing and recycling water; any other fuel was hoarded for Bravo Rising's weapons and their small fleet of starfighters, stolen or borrowed from Atterra's disbanded security forces.

Rose and Paige and their pilot guide sat in the center of the wide atrium as the focus of the gathering, along with Orion Chalk. Rose wondered if they'd have to make a speech to the people there. This was not something she felt confident about. She didn't think Paige did, either.

But Reeve Panzoro, running on adrenaline, was proving himself fiercely in control.

"We need a plan to take back to General Organa," he said. "A *specific* plan. Ms. Casca's convinced Leia to give us help, and the general has sent Paige and Rose as her emissaries to work out how they'll get through the blockade and where they should land."

"Slow down. You just blasted from zero to lightspeed," Rose protested. "We're only here to make sure your story's true. And if it is, Leia *might* be able to send support."

"You know it's true," Reeve insisted. "You saw the death transport! And now that you're here—"

"Now that we're here, it's clearer how we can help," Paige said. "We can offer you a plan."

Rose backed her up, teasing, "Paige likes to plan parties."

"Sure I do," said Paige. "The Old Lady had a suggestion that would work. We can use the StarFortress bombers to make supply runs here."

Rose, remembering what Fossil had said, agreed. "We wouldn't even have to land. We could send loaded shells in as a drop to a few designated sites." She turned to look at Paige. "We could rig other StarFortresses with power bafflers like the one in *Hammer*. If we got other people besides me working on it, we could set them up pretty quickly. It's not hard to do; it's just tedious wiring up all the circuits. Those asteroids in the Atterra Belt mean it's really easy to stay out of sight, and if all the bombers get their power covered up, we should be able to come and go pretty safely—"

"Just as long as we don't run into too many of those automatic cannons," Paige reminded her.

"But we can help with those," said Orion Chalk, Reeve's uncle, the one who'd threatened them with the solar crossbow when they'd first arrived. "We've mapped hundreds of them. Reeve Panzoro's father was part of the team that works on that. And we can show you how to avoid the minefields."

"The only thing is, it might have to be a very short party," Rose said apologetically. She knew how slender the Resistance resources were, and she didn't think that Leia would be able to keep this blockade-running plan going for long. It was going to have to be an operation that enabled the Atterrans to mount their own defense, just as Casca Panzoro had suggested.

Paige was thinking the same thing.

"What do you need most?" she asked.

All around her voices began to speak up. She heard several different answers, but Rose could tell that the Bravo Rising assembly was unanimous about one thing in particular.

"Water."

"What we need most is *water.*"

"Fuel—weapons—power to fight back. But we can't do anything without water. *What we need most is water.*"

"We've always farmed it ourselves on Bravo," explained Orion Chalk. "But when the gas extraction industry began here, the population expanded so much that it's been hundreds of years since we've been self-sufficient in drinkable water. We count on shipments from Atterra Alpha. Since our water's been blockaded, at least half the planet has died—quickly. It only took a week or two after the water started to run out."

"Where do you get it now?"

"The Firestone Islands contain most of Bravo's hydro farms. Until the large ones were taken over by the First Order, we supplied water to townships all over the northern quadrant. We may not have access to those farms anymore, but several people in the Big Settlement are self-sufficient backyard water farmers. That's why Bravo Rising is centered here." Chalk took a deep breath. "We've been smuggling water to other settlements, but we've barely got enough to keep the survivors alive. If we could take out the patrols that blockade this section, we'd be able to take back the main Firestone Island water supply."

"We need to arrange drop points," said Paige. "If you can provide us with those locations, information about the automatic cannons and minefields, and a list of other supplies that will help you pull off your defense, we can take those back to our crew and get this ball rolling within a week. We'll find a way to run through this blockade."

And suddenly, it looked like it was really going to happen. Paige and Rose were going to become blockade runners.

————

Armed with information that all the probe droids in the galaxy could not have uncovered for them, Paige and Rose left late the following morning to head back to the *Little Vixen*.

They'd expected Reeve to come with them. *Reeve* had expected to go with them. But apparently no one else had expected it.

"Reeve Panzoro!" Orion Chalk stopped him in the middle of strapping up his pack. "You're not *leaving*? But you—"

"I've got to get back to Ms. Casca," Reeve objected quickly. "I've got to report to her."

"The emissaries will report to her. That's what they

came to do—to check out her story. But we need you here—without Ms. Casca, you're the only Panzoro we've got!"

"But—" Reeve sounded panicked. Rose could tell that he'd been expecting to be reunited with his grandmother the moment they returned to D'Qar.

"She's our leader, and you're *her* representative," said Chalk. "Of course you're free to make your own decision, but I hope you'll stay. We need you here."

Reeve had been separated from Casca Panzoro forcefully; he hadn't chosen to leave her on D'Qar. But now he was being given a choice.

Reeve's face twisted. He looked torn apart. "But she thinks I'm coming back," he said.

"You're our only link with this bomber group," Chalk insisted. "They'll need you here as a contact. Your experience with their leaders and equipment will be vital to us if anything goes wrong with their mission."

Rose watched Reeve Panzoro with the familiar feeling of sympathy. She knew he was terrified of the blockade. He was terrified of dying of thirst, or worse, in this hostile place that had once been his home. She remembered the fearful relief on his face when he'd climbed out of the ship he'd crash-landed in the belly of the StarFortress.

But she knew that he was bolder and more determined than she'd taken him for when she'd first met him. She remembered how he'd come up with the ruse that had helped them escape the ship that was hunting them when they'd arrived on Atterra Bravo. She remembered how he'd run into the open on the pumice beach, risking his life to bring back her canteen so that the First Order transport wouldn't notice it.

Rose kept her lips clamped shut. She couldn't blame him for being loyal to his grandmother. She knew that if she were Reeve and Casca were Paige, Rose would choose to go back to her sister every time.

Rose saw now, uncomfortably, that this might not be the right choice.

She didn't dare join in this debate.

But Paige suddenly did.

"You're always thinking about your grandmother's instructions," she said to Reeve. "What would she tell you now?"

Chalk turned to look at her with respect. Reeve, when he looked at Paige himself, still wore an expression of unhappy indecision.

"What would Casca want you to do?" Paige asked in her calm, fearless, tail-gunner-under-fire voice.

Reeve Panzoro swallowed. Then, suddenly, he gave a sharp nod.

"She'd want me to do the job I was needed for." He paused. "So would my father."

"Well, then," Paige said with satisfaction. "There you go."

Reeve took a deep breath. He closed his eyes. Rose could imagine what he was thinking.

She's the only one I have left. If I do this, I might never see her again.

And then he made his decision, knowing that now he was going to be able to navigate new uncharted stars alone.

"All right. I'll stay. I'll do it."

Nothing, Rose thought, *is as peaceful as the limitless blue of hyperspace.*

She and Paige hadn't wasted any time getting out of the Atterra system. They'd taken off as soon as they reached the *Vixen,* and before the end of a twenty-four-hour time block, Rose and Paige were once again alone in the suspended reality following the jump to lightspeed.

Paige leaned back in the pilot's seat, stretching. "*Wow*—what a terrible place. Not really what we meant about seeing the galaxy." She touched her Haysian ore medallion.

Seeing Paige's fingers straying to her throat, Rose mirrored her sister's action. The familiar wave of love and connection washed over her. They were both touching a little bit of Otomok at the same time—two halves that made a whole—a reminder of the cause they were fighting for, and a physical link to their lost home.

"Do you think there *is* any place out there that's beautiful and . . ." Rose paused. She'd been going to say *peaceful*, but it didn't really seem to be the right word. Without human habitation, Atterra Bravo would have been a place of beauty and peace. But adding *people* into the mix changed it completely.

"And what?"

"A good place for a picnic," Rose said. "Never mind. There must be somewhere. It was a stupid question."

Paige set the autopilot. Hyperspace was a relief after Atterra. She stood up in the little cabin and unrolled a couple of blankets. She grinned at Rose.

"Hyperspace is beautiful," said Paige. "And we can picnic right here."

She spread out the blankets and arranged the insulated mug and protein packets as if she and Rose were galactic nobility on a feast day. "Come on, Rose—sit down and let's look at the map. Let's plan our interstellar vacation."

"You are ridiculous," Rose grumbled.

They wrapped up close together in the blankets, sharing each other's warmth. Right now, this was home.

Rose had a sudden mental image of the pair of them cocooned together all alone, surrounded by light-years and light-years of empty space, as if they were the only two people alive in the entire galaxy—or at least the only two people who mattered.

But of course there were a lot of other desperate people out there. As if to remind them, Paige pulled up a miniature map of the Outer Rim.

"D'Qar is too far from Atterra to make a regular series of supply runs efficiently," she said. "We need to find a place to use as an intermediate base for the heavy bomber unit. Leia had a suggestion for a planet we could check out, just in case. There."

Paige pointed.

Only a short hyperspace jump from Atterra, there was a world on the edge of a mostly uninhabited star system. It was marked "Industrial" and "Independent."

"'Refnu,'" Rose read aloud. "How come Leia tells you all this extra stuff?"

"Insurance. If we're both caught, only one of us knows anything."

The implication made Rose shiver. "That's not exactly reassuring," she said, uncomfortably glad to let her older sister take on the burden of being the one who risked having information tortured out of her. In defense of her own secret selfishness, Rose said quickly, "Now we both know."

"But we won't get caught," Paige said, squeezing Rose's hand. "One of the other StarFortress techs suggested it to us—he grew up on Refnu. Cat, the big guy. You know which one I mean, the bomber *Treasure*'s flight engineer?

Anyway, Leia thinks that operating out of Refnu will be good cover. It won't be too far for our Forts to go back and forth between Refnu and Atterra. It's in a good position for us to load the supplies we'll need. And there's no real reason for anyone to trace the bombers back to D'Qar or to the Resistance. It'll look like someone on Refnu is being a good neighbor to Atterra. Shall we stop in on our way home?"

"What, without even asking Leia? Or Fossil? Just drop in on a strange planet and say hi?"

"Traveling the galaxy together," Paige reminded her. "I've been given a pile of credits to negotiate some docking berths for the Forts if we're going to go ahead with this."

Rose couldn't help laughing. "Traveling with you is not turning out like I expected. But then, neither is the galaxy."

"The galaxy's great," said Paige, and they both laughed.

―――――――

Neither Paige nor Rose was prepared for the deep, agonizing homesickness that slammed them during their brief trip to Refnu.

It wasn't exactly like Hays Minor in the Otomok system. But it was the most like it of any place they'd been since they left home.

Rose had felt a kind of fierce loyalty to the Atterras

just because they were twin worlds. Now she found herself feeling the same kind of loyalty to Refnu, because she understood it.

Cold and dark, Refnu was as far out on the edge of its habitable zone as the Hays worlds had been, and—like Hays Minor—Refnu was barely warm enough to support life. The planet was so far from its sun that it existed in perpetual twilight. From the minute Paige set down their craft on the windy, frost-rimmed spaceport on Refnu, both she and Rose had felt as though they were finally coming home.

They couldn't get out of their little Resistance ship at first. They weren't dressed for it. After a bit of wrangling over the comm with someone who called himself the "harbormaster" in a puffed-up way, a crane trundled over to them through the purple twilight and deposited a thermal dome over the *Vixen* so they wouldn't freeze to death when they climbed out. Then a couple of dockworkers brought them weathersuits.

It was exactly the way a strange ship would have been welcomed on Hays Minor. Paige caught Rose's eye as they climbed into the weathersuits and gave her a bright little encouraging half smile. Rose knew her sister was feeling the same sense of bittersweet nostalgia.

Life had never been easy on Hays Minor—but that was no reason for it to be *destroyed*.

Paige and Rose spent only one night on Refnu. They

weren't exactly welcomed, as they'd been on Atterra Bravo. They had to rent their weathersuits by the hour and pay for a bunk in the freighters' barracks in order to stay on the planet's surface. It seemed strange to be back in a place where paying for services from strangers was a normal thing to do.

Leia's New Republic credits were welcomed, and Paige reluctantly spent them. The weathersuits and a place to sleep were necessities if they wanted to survive the harshness of Refnu's climate.

"But you can't just slap down a pile of cash and buy docking space for a couple of squadrons of heavy Fort bombers," Rose pointed out to her older sister.

"Of course not. The Resistance can't afford it, for one thing. And for another, it would look incredibly suspicious."

"So what are you going to do, Intelligence?"

Paige laughed. "Reconnaissance! I said we'll *negotiate*. Remember my job back home on Hays Minor?"

"You were not a diplomat," Rose reminded her. "You were an ore digger pilot for the Central Ridge Mining Company."

"I bet they need icebreakers here, too, just like they did on Hays Minor," Paige said. "And I bet they wouldn't say no to an experienced bomber squadron who could do it for them. I think we should go eat supper with the other freighters."

09

IT REMINDED Rose *so much* of Hays Minor that it made her chest hurt. She thought she could actually feel the heartache.

The freighters' canteen was a long, windowless hall bright with artificial daylight. There were no windows—just like home. In a world where it was always dark and almost always stormy, windows were pointless. The light from the plasma ceiling reminded Rose piercingly of the heart of her family living pod, the tiny bright space the Ticos had called the "sunroom." Every residential space on Hays Minor had been equipped with a sunroom of some kind. The artificial light was necessary to sustain life.

"A snowgrape vine!" Paige gasped, pointing.

"All this way to see a snowgrape vine!" Rose laughed. But she grasped her older sister's hand and squeezed hard.

The vine was big—it must have been over a hundred years old. It was a lot like the one that had twisted around the small domed space of their own sunroom, every tiny sour fruit closely monitored by the pod superintendent and any harvest shared across four communal kitchens. The old vine hadn't belonged to the Ticos, but they'd been the lucky family who got to sit beneath its pale green foliage and spicy blossoms. Its teardrop-shaped leaves echoed the shape of the pale gold medallions Paige and Rose wore and treasured, the matched gift from their parents just before they'd fled the Otomok system.

This vine in the freighters' canteen on Refnu was in a cage—precious enough to warrant protection from anyone who would carelessly or greedily disturb its carefully coaxed fruits.

Paige and Rose picked up food trays at a serving hatch and managed to get seats at one of the long bench tables not far from the vine's green fragrance. When they sat down, Paige laughed in delight. "Look—selakale!"

In narrow trenches down the center of the table, pale sprouts were growing under the artificial light. Back on Hays Minor in the Otomok system, selakale had been a valuable vitamin source, but you had to strip the seeds from it and replant them daily or you'd have nothing to eat the next day. Here, you could help yourself and replant as you ate.

"I like this place," said Paige happily, piling the bitter shoots on top of her steaming portion of starch rations and poking the seeds back into the soil trench.

The other travelers sitting nearby laughed at her enthusiasm.

"You from around here?" rumbled one of them, humanoid but gigantic. "But no—I don't think so. You're too small to be a Refnu native. Look at me, Dario the Nefrian—my extra skin layer keeps me warm. And my bones are bigger to hold the extra weight. Where are you from, then?"

"Otomok, originally," said Paige. "A planet called Hays Minor. Same climate. No native intelligent life there, though."

This got another laugh.

"Call Dario intelligent life?" teased another Nefrian.

"Well, you couldn't like the climate on this iceberg if you weren't used to it, that's for sure!" said someone else.

Rose saw what Paige had done: attracted attention on purpose by making people interested in her story, but also by putting the strangers at ease right away.

How does she do it? Rose wondered. *And could I ever do it without her—could I ever feel so confident on my own, not knowing any of these people?*

"What brings you to this dark snowball?" asked a scaly, lizard-like humanoid sitting across from them, shivering in his weathersuit with taloned hands wrapped around a hot mug. "Not the climate, for sure."

"We're looking for work. Freelance ice bombers—we

fly in a converted StarFortress. Figured this place was as good as any," Paige said.

"You've worked in frozen ore extraction?" asked Dario, the big guy. "You're here at a good time. It's summer."

This brought hoots of laughter from the lizard person, who obviously wasn't from around these parts. *"Summer!"*

"Yeah, summer, you sunbug. That means the days are long up north, and you can clear the ice away from the surface for a little while so you can get to the minerals underneath. What's your name, miss?"

"Paige. Paige Tico—this is my sister, Rose."

The folk around the table nodded greetings.

"I know that RefnuCorp hires extra workers this time of year," said Dario. "Check in at their HQ. It's tunnel seventeen-eighty-two, and you don't have to go outside to get there. I'm not sure one StarFortress is going to be much good to them, though."

"Oh, we're just the reconnaissance party," Paige said, grinning.

Rose kicked her. Paige didn't bat an eyelash.

"We're here in advance of the rest of the crew," Paige said. "Checking out the lay of the land. What a waste of energy and time and fuel it would have been if we'd all flown out to the back end of nowhere and then discovered we couldn't get work! We can offer RefnuCorp a full squadron if they want it."

Back on D'Qar, Leia was cautiously enthusiastic about the Tico sisters' report.

"We can run four supply hops," she said firmly.

She and a fellow Resistance officer, Vice-Admiral Amilyn Holdo, were laying the groundwork for the mission with all the members of the heavy bomber unit: Fossil, sixty crew, and another sixty ground staff who would go along to Refnu to take over the refueling, maintenance, and loading work for the flight crews when they came back to base.

"Holdo's had experience with airlift missions before," Leia explained. "She won't be going along with you, but I've asked her to listen in on our plans."

Holdo was a serene woman of about Leia's age, thin and tall, with purple hair. She was in command of the cruiser *Ninka*. She stood on one side of Leia while Casca Panzoro stood on the other side as their consultant. The three older women made a formidable trio.

Leia had spent hours in private conversation with Casca and Holdo, but this was the first time their plans were being revealed.

"We can't afford to supply Atterra Bravo with more than four airlift runs," Leia continued. "We don't have a contact on Atterra Alpha and we'd better limit ourselves to communicating with Bravo Rising. We'll have to be careful about the timing, too; we don't want to attract a lot of attention.

"We can send eleven StarFortress bombers in all, with eleven full crews. Seven of Cobalt Squadron will go, along with four from Crimson. That way six bombers can head to Atterra and five can work for the Refnu Corporation each day. Finch Dallow of Cobalt will lead both squadrons to Atterra. Finch, you think you have a good idea of how to avoid the minefields?"

"Well, I hope so," said Finch.

"That's the best we can do," said Leia. "Are you all with me?"

She looked around, watching people nod their acknowledgment and understanding.

"Good," Leia said. "So. Amilyn, can you add to what I've said?"

"We'll stock the bombers for the first two runs before you leave, and we'll send a transport with you with full clips of supplies for the third and fourth runs," Holdo told them. "You'll probably need to send the transport back here for your final fuel supply. But you'll be on your own on Refnu."

"Try to juggle things so it doesn't look like you're racing off on a rescue mission in your spare time, okay?" Leia added. "Don't forget you're supposed to be icebreakers."

One of the pilots raised a hand. "Won't it be obvious

what the rest of us are doing while the decoy squadron's busy mining?"

"Use a cover story," Leia told him, ever the diplomat. "You're making the most of your time and working a delivery service on your days off. Cat, the flight engineer on the bomber *Treasure*, knows the planet and the system; he's the reason you heard there might be work there."

Leia paused and made a face at the questioner.

"Just don't make it obvious where you're heading," she warned.

The next forty-eight hours evaporated in a whirl of preparations. Vice-Admiral Holdo and Fossil consulted Casca Panzoro on what was most urgently needed in the bombers' payloads and in the supplementary supplies carried in the biggest transport available. The bomber crews supervised the ground crews and double-checked all the ships' equipment in preparation for the mission.

Rose scarcely slept. She had the task of overseeing eleven teams as they wired up each of the StarFortress bombers with power-reducing bafflers like the one in *Hammer*.

"Come on."

It was Paige's voice.

Paige had found her sister sitting against the grass of the camouflaged bunker wall. Rose was in between power checks, taking a five-minute break to rehydrate and *breathe*.

Fresh air. The only way to get at the awkward power bafflers was by crawling underneath and sitting up inside them on the flight decks of the heavy bombers. It was claustrophobic at the best of times; with two people, Rose plus the flight engineer she was supervising, it was stifling. The StarFortresses were on low power for ground maintenance, and it was stuffy and hot inside them. By the end of an hour Rose had stripped down to her tank top, and that was drenched. The Otomok medallion swung free, and kept catching on the baffler plugs.

Rose was glad of a break after a day of this.

Paige snagged her by the arm where she was resting against the outside grass-covered wall of the bunker.

"Come on, let's take a quick walk."

"I haven't got time. I just wanted to get some air."

"If you've got time to sit there, you've got time for a walk," Paige said. "It'll be dark soon anyway. You'll feel better if you get moving."

Rose let herself be led.

The light was different late in the day than it was in early morning. The birds were quiet.

"On some planets," said Paige, "where there's a huge variety of wildlife and they have big animals as well as little flying things, there are nocturnal animals, too. What animal would you *most* like to see?"

"Anything as long as I don't have to herd it." Rose didn't feel like playing this game, and the darkening trees seemed ominous to her.

"I'd choose fathiers," Paige said. "If I could only see one animal in the whole galaxy, and I'd never get to see anything else, I'd go for fathiers. I'd like to see them in a race. I'd like to *ride* one—"

"Paige," Rose interrupted, "could you be quiet about animals right now?"

She shivered. Now that she was out in the open and could feel the wind on her skin, she was no longer sweating. She wished she'd put her overalls back on before she headed off duty.

Paige laid her arm over Rose's shoulders and held her close.

"I *thought* something was bothering you. What are you worrying about?"

"You always know."

For a moment they stood there, quiet together—it was getting too late now to go any farther into the alien forest. But in another moment they'd have to turn back, and then there would hardly be any more time together until—when? Until they were back in hyperspace on the way to another bombing mission, riding doubled up in the lower gun ball turret?

"Okay," Rose said. "Here's the thing. You know I'm supervising the installation of these power-reducing bafflers in the Forts for this mission? Well, wiring them up is a pain, and I can't do it all myself. I have to go around and make sure that other people are doing the right thing. And mostly they are. Sometimes I see something that's out of place, and I point it out, and they fix it."

"So what's the problem?" Paige asked. "Is someone being sloppy? Or aren't we going to be ready in time?"

"No, no, nothing like that. Everybody's working really hard. And we're ahead of schedule."

Rose shivered again.

"Well, what then?"

"I'm worried the bafflers won't work," said Rose.

"But ours worked fine!"

"Sure it did." Rose hesitated again, then finally managed to spit out what was bothering her. "But if one single plug were out of place, and it made the baffler in one of the other Forts fail, and they got spotted by a TIE fighter patrol, it would be *my fault* if everybody on that bomber ended up dead."

Paige was silent.

"It was bad enough worrying about Reeve—just one

person—when we had to take him along. But this is me having to be responsible for the *whole squadron*."

When a few more seconds passed and Paige still didn't say anything, Rose added brazenly, trying to brush past the moment, "Of course, if our baffler fails first, I guess I won't have to worry about—"

Paige stopped her with one word.

"*Rose.*"

Rose didn't turn to look at her sister, ashamed of her own uncertainty, ashamed of getting *anything* wrong when Paige was always so calm and controlled.

"Rose, we're in this *together*," Paige said. "If a pilot doesn't fly fast enough, or doesn't get over the drop zone in exactly the right place, or the bombardier is a second late making the release, or the tail gunner doesn't hit every bandit she fires at, do we all sit around blaming them?"

She began to walk back toward the base, steering Rose under her warm, familiar arm.

"You know we don't," Paige continued. "That's what it is to be a soldier. And we're at war. Maybe it's not a great big heroic intergalactic conflict like when the Empire was defeated, and maybe we're not at the center of it. But we're part of an effort. We're making a *difference*. And maybe we're going to give Atterra a chance that Otomok didn't get."

She squeezed Rose's shoulder.

"And that's something that won't happen without taking some risks," Paige finished. "Without taking some *responsibility.*"

When Rose still didn't answer, Paige prompted her.

"Say I'm right!"

Rose gave a grudging little laugh. "You're always right, Pae-Pae."

"That's because I'm older and I know best."

"Ha ha."

Rose knew that Paige *was* right. And yet, she also knew that if something went wrong with one of those power bafflers and Rose wasn't there to fix it *herself,* she was going to feel guilty about it for the rest of her life.

———

It didn't take the StarFortress unit long to get set up on Refnu. They wasted no more than a day working out a settlement with the Refnu Corporation for the wharf space and the icebreaking work. Then they readied the bombers for their first assignments and collapsed in their bunk space with the other temporary workers.

Early the next morning, five of the eleven heavy bombers were fitted with bomb clips packed full of icebreaking equipment, and they set off lumbering northward into

Refnu's frozen ore zones for the work mission they'd promised RefnuCorp.

The other six Resistance bombers, four from the Cobalt Squadron supported by two from Crimson, weren't carrying magno-charge explosives. They were headed for the Atterra system, and this time, instead of spy equipment, their bomb racks contained shell cases filled with thousands of liters of water and portable condensers; vehicle fuel; flour, protein packs, tins of smoked cloudfish, vitamin supplements, and medical supplies; and an assortment of electronic and mechanical equipment, including several hyperdrive compressors for small ships, lightspeed radio receivers, and energy cells for ammunition.

The StarFortress bombers carried the first delivery of an airlift that would give Bravo Rising the self-sufficiency it needed to fight for independence for the twin Atterra worlds.

———

Paige glanced at the chrono on her wrist. "Ten minutes to realspace. You need to be at the tech monitor when we enter the Atterra system. Go poke Nix and Spennie on your way."

"Okay," Rose said. "See you again on the way back to Refnu."

She said it casually, as if they weren't about to sneak six Resistance StarFortresses through a First Order blockade.

Paige was equally casual. She gave the same response she always gave at the beginning of a bombing run. "See you then, Rose."

Rose boosted herself off the back of the gunner's seat and into the bomb bay. She closed the shield door to the gunner's turret behind her, sealing Paige in. Then Rose made her way up the long ladder past the bomb racks to the flight deck.

Rose shivered all over again as she climbed past the thousands of black and shining shells.

Nuts and bolts, she swore to herself. *What's the matter with you, Rose? They aren't even bombs! They're full of protein snacks and antiseptic wipes!*

But of course there was ammunition in there, too, and they still *looked* like bombs. For a moment, Rose couldn't help wishing they were all magno-charge explosives after all, and that they were going to be used in a real attack— something that would stop the First Order once and for all.

Rose waved up at the bombardier. "Hey, Nix. Paige said to give you a poke."

Nix was sitting by his computer pedestal with his legs swinging over the edge of the opening to the bomb bay, running a last count of the active racks from the handheld remote detonator. Nix raised his head and nodded in reply to Rose, but he didn't answer or let go of the remote. Rose knew he was doing his usual careful tally of the shells before he activated their release.

"Five minutes to entry," Rose warned him. "Don't lose count now."

Nix nodded again without a word. He was always totally focused on the mission. Rose thought it was probably his way of coping with the lurking coil of fear.

Everybody coped with it differently. Rose reached the upper deck and went to check on Spennie, the new tail gunner. They'd managed to fill out each bomber with a full crew of five for this hop, which would free up the flight engineer to keep an eye on the power bafflers.

Hammer's crew had flown with Spennie once or twice before as a tail gunner, enough that they all knew she spent her time in hyperspace listening to Coruscant space-race broadcasts mostly recorded a hundred years before. Rose squeezed past the grotesque hulk of the baffler and bent down into the tail turret. There Spennie sat, rapt in her own dreamworld, pretending she was speeding across the solar system in a sleek solar yacht of a bygone age.

Rose tapped on Spennie's headset. "Paige said—"

Rose cut herself short. In her head she heard Reeve Panzoro accusing her: *You don't do anything without making sure it's okay with Paige.* She sounded just as child-ish as Reeve going on about what his grandmother had told him to do.

"I'm here with your three-minute warning, Spennie," Rose amended.

"Thanks." The tail gunner reached up to change channels with one hand, and with the other began the unlocking sequence for her guns. "Seal me in, okay?"

"I'm on it."

Rose ducked back out to the main deck and closed the shield door to the tail gunner's turret.

"Tech, take your station." Finch Dallow's voice in her headset was sharp. He was playing the professional pilot for once. "Navicomputer's ready for reentry. Expect the unexpected."

10

ROSE GLANCED at her chrono—she'd been one minute too long on the ladder through the bomb racks, staring at those ominous black canisters.

Now she wriggled her way back around the baffler and sprinted across the flight deck, her boots clattering hollowly over the hard-used panels. She took her seat at the flight engineer's console. Her job on this trip was going to be considerably more nerve-racking than it had been on the first bombing run to Atterra, with the spy droids: this time, instead of just monitoring her own ship, she was responsible for overseeing all six of the mission squadron's power bafflers.

Rose barely had time to get her retaining straps fastened before *Hammer* was out of hyperspace and cruising in the clear space on the far side of the Atterra Belt. Before Rose knew it, Finch had covered the distance between reentry and the asteroids, and then *Hammer* began dodging and hiding in Atterra's rock-filled space maze.

Rose looked at her screen. If the power bafflers were all working, they'd hide the energy trace from the bombers. That meant Rose would see the StarFortresses as outlines on her screen, only able to see them fully if they were in her own ship's line of sight.

At the tech station, Rose had no actual view of what was going on outside the ship. All she could see were the outlined asteroids of the belt. She scanned the screen, searching for an outline in the awkward pistol shape of a Resistance StarFortress. The bombers only oriented themselves all in the same position when they were flying in formation, so they might appear any way up on her screen during this run, making the shapes themselves hard to spot.

It was a bit like doing one of those visual puzzles Paige had liked so much when they were kids—finding the outlines of off-world animals among a big jumble of abstract shapes.

Big animals, these heavy bombers, Rose thought, letting herself smile. *Probably the closest thing to a fathier that Paige or I will ever get to ride on.*

Then Rose spotted another ship from Cobalt Squadron. It was a little behind the bomber *Hammer,* following the same path into Atterra Bravo's orbit, skirting the edge of one of the Atterra Belt's asteroids.

Paige called up from the lower ball turret, where she was facing rearward. She'd seen the other StarFortress, too.

"One of ours behind us, Finch."

"Cobalt Squadron and Crimson support ships, check in," Rose heard Finch command over the comm system. She couldn't hear their responses, but she heard Finch acknowledging each. None was very far away from *Hammer*.

"Sorry to hear about that, Cobalt *Mare*," Rose heard Finch say. "Which of these lumps of rock had the automatic cannon?"

In another few seconds Finch read back a number for Rose to log.

"*Mare* got fired at," Finch explained. "No damage. Listen, kids, we can't regroup in the belt, and if we trigger any more of those automatic cannons, we're going to attract attention. Let's head straight for Atterra, form up, drop, and get out of here as fast as we can. We'll come in on the dark side."

"The dark side!" Nix snorted with laughter. "Are we turning to evil?"

"The *night* side, you idiot. Of the *planet*."

They made their way across the Atterra Belt to the open space within its giant ring. Ahead of them, Atterra Bravo glowed bravely on Rose's screen—bright, barren, bleak, and ruined. After the cold, familiar dark of Refnu, Rose was reminded again how hard on her eyes she'd found the brightness of an inner planet when she'd first escaped her twilit home on Hays Minor back in ruined Otomok.

Somewhere on the other side of the sun, she knew, was Atterra Bravo's sister, Atterra Alpha. No one could ever see both worlds at once.

In the same way, somewhere far below in the bomber *Hammer*, Rose knew, was her own sister.

"All our bombers are out of the belt," Rose reported as the gold traces appeared and began to converge on her monitor. "Welcome to Atterra, everybody!"

"Cobalt Squadron, Crimson support ships, join formation and proceed to drop point," she heard Finch command. "Follow me. As far as I know we're coming in between mine zones, but keep a good lookout. And watch for bandits."

The warning had been to alert the other bombers, but *Hammer*'s crew took it personally.

"Looking," came Paige's voice, and then Spennie's voice from the tail gun turret echoed, "Looking."

In the back of her mind, Rose remembered how the

TIE fighters had appeared on her monitor, sparks of twinkling white heat like shooting stars.

Scanning the monitor, she thought that there was nothing in the galaxy she dreaded as much as the anticipation of seeing those searing handfuls of glitter suddenly appear on-screen.

"Empty sky, Nix," said the pilot to the bombardier. "We might get a straight run. Entering atmosphere—drop in ten."

"Copy," said Nix.

Rose knew that silence from the flight engineer was considered good news, so she didn't say anything.

She sat tense and aching with her eyes glued to the screen. She watched as the image of the world grew vastly closer in the monitor, until the bombers were so close to Atterra Bravo that she couldn't see its spherical outline anymore.

Before her eyes, the planet rapidly changed from a distant world into a shadowy landscape. From space, Atterra Bravo had glowed in the reflected light of its sun. But on its nighttime surface, all was dark.

Rose had noticed that even in the perpetual twilight of Refnu, there was always some pinpoint of light beckoning through the gloom—landing lights on the wharfs, beacon signals along the ground routes between the mines, warning lights on top of cranes and other obstacles to sky traffic. Refnu was too far from its sun for its surfaces to glitter. But even in a world where there were no windows, unless the surface was obliterated by cloud, there was always some small flame of life glowing to guide a flight crew in to land.

As *Hammer* approached Atterra Bravo, Rose knew that the sky outside was full of starlight. But on her screen, the surface of the besieged planet was dead with darkness.

The first drop zone was in a steep depression three kilometers across. It could have been an open mine or a bomb crater—from looking at her screen it was impossible to tell which. An empty shell of a city loomed around it in the darkness, with mining rigs snapped off and tossed down the slopes of the crater; there was no light in any window, no sign of life among the towering ruins.

Rose knew there was life down there. She'd seen it herself. She'd met the people who were struggling to keep this planet from going under. Somewhere below her, Reeve Panzoro was looking up at the sky with his frightened young heart full of desperate determination.

But from above, it didn't look as if Atterra Bravo had any chance of survival.

We're their hope, Rose reminded herself. *Cobalt Squadron is why they're looking up at the sky. They know we're coming and they're waiting for us.*

Rose watched the outlines of the other StarFortresses, now lined up in formation on her screen, all of them speeding toward the lightless drop point on Atterra Bravo.

"Drop point in five," came Finch's terse update.

"Copy," Nix repeated.

The bomber *Hammer* swooped lower over the target. Rose imagined what Paige and Spennie must be seeing, crammed in their crystal spheres behind the laser cannons and nervously watching the brilliant asteroid-littered sky behind them: that was where an attack was most likely to come from.

"They don't use lights at night," Paige said. They were close enough to the planet that Rose knew her sister could see it through the clear panes beneath her feet. She, too, had noticed the unnatural darkness of Atterra Bravo. "I guess the First Order would dive in for a recruitment sweep the second they spotted a sign of life here. Not to mention resistance . . ."

"Quit chatting, kids, the sky's clear," said Finch. "Here we go. Nix, you ready with those bomb bay doors?"

Suddenly, on Rose's screen, one of the glowing gold StarFortress outlines on the port side of the formation flickered and flashed solid features.

Rose caught her breath before speaking. She didn't want to worry anyone unnecessarily.

But then it happened again, and she could see the

other bomber clearly on the screen, fully visible as a power source burning energy.

Rose swallowed. She could hardly speak around the lump of dread in her throat.

"*Treasure*'s baffler—Cobalt *Treasure*'s baffler is down," she managed to croak. "You'd better break the bad news to them, Finch."

She added miserably, *"I'm sorry."*

"Cobalt *Treasure*, it's Cobalt *Hammer* here. We're holding for you. Go on in first." *Hammer*'s crew could hear the command Finch gave. "Then get out as fast as you can and don't hang around for the rest of us."

It wasn't too different from the original plan. *Hammer* had intended to lead the way, with the other bombers following. Each StarFortress was supposed to make its own way back without waiting for the others, except for *Hammer*—*Hammer* would watch to make sure the drop went according to plan. That way Rose would be around to give advice in case of a power baffler failure.

She really hadn't expected that failure to happen so early in the game.

Rose watched her screen. She could see the outline of her own ship falling back behind the others to let the vulnerable one go first, to give them a chance to make their drop as quickly as possible and streak away for the safety of hyperspace.

Rose swallowed again. Then she took a deep breath.

"Finch, patch me in to *Treasure*'s flight engineer," she said. She had her own general comm so she could talk to all the other StarFortress technicians at once, but she wanted a private link to Cat.

She heard her pilot punching in the sequence. The seconds ticked by. Rose couldn't believe how time suddenly seemed to crawl during the minutes it took them to approach the target, especially now that one of the Resistance bombers was visible to the entire solar system of Atterra if anyone happened to be watching.

"*Treasure* tech, it's Rose here," Rose said. "Your baffler's spewing power. Can I help?"

Cat, the technician from Refnu, didn't answer right away. Rose could hear him breathing hard. She could feel her own breath choking her as she waited, a feeling of panic.

"Take another deep breath, Rose."

Through Rose's headset came Paige's calm voice, as though her sister were speaking right beside her, telling her what to do.

"Take a deep breath, then prompt him."

Rose breathed deep.

She tried to imagine Cat, with his large Nefrian build, crammed inside the cone of *Treasure*'s power baffler. What would he be looking at? What was wrong?

"Hey, Cat. If it's not obvious what's wrong, you have to check all the connections. There's a sequence. I can talk you through it."

"We're thirty seconds from the drop," came the *Treasure* flight engineer's voice. "I can't do this now."

———

Rose could do nothing but watch the screen while the bomber *Treasure* released the first delivery of the Atterra airlift.

The shells that carried the emergency supplies didn't have power bafflers or guidance systems. They simply relied on gravity, like ancient weaponry. *Hammer*, having switched places with *Treasure*, was brief minutes behind the other StarFortress. Even so close, the shells were invisible on Rose's monitors. She could only assume that *Treasure* had been able to make its release—the first batch of the water, food, fuel, weaponry, and medical supplies that the Atterrans so desperately needed.

Treasure swung away from the drop, and *Hammer* took its place.

For a couple of seconds over the target, Rose flipped the primary monitor to interior so she could watch the bomb bay doors opening. Nix was on the job and the doors were working smoothly.

In agony over what was going on with *Treasure*'s power baffler, Rose flipped the screen back to exterior so she could see the other bomber.

Treasure was on its way back out into Atterra Bravo's orbit now. Its pilot was trying to stay within the dark of the planet's night. Once they reached orbit, it would be all too easy to overshoot and end up in daylight.

"*Treasure* tech? Cat? You ready for me to hold your hand?" Rose called across space.

"I'm sorry, Rose," came Cat's voice. "I'm so, so sorry. It's all my fault!"

He was still panting.

"One of our bomb grips had seized up, and I'd gone down into the racks to help the bombardier loosen it so it would release for the drop, and then after I came up the ladder to the flight deck again I forgot to turn off my traction gloves. Just after we got out of hyperspace, I thought—I thought I should check the plugs in the baffler, and I climbed inside it, and I touched the plugs, and about a dozen of them stuck to the gloves and just pulled right out of the power wall! And then—"

Rose realized, from the clicking and rattling that was going on in the background, that Cat was rapidly reconnecting plugs as he spoke to her.

"And then I sort of grabbed at them with my other hand to stop them falling, instinctively I guess, and I pulled out another half a dozen by accident."

"Oh, *Cat*." Rose sighed—partly out of frustration and partly, secretly, out of relief. This hadn't been her fault after all.

"Wish I could have been there to *literally* hold your hand," she said.

Cat gave a quick, sharp bark of laughter. "I'll sit on my hands next time."

"You going to get this fixed any time soon?" Rose asked. "I want to help you check the sequencing, but we're about to make our own drop."

"I'm on it, Rose. Call me when you're done and I'll read you what I've got."

"Thanks, Cat."

Rose focused on her screen. The bomb bay doors were standing open.

Then the edge of the screen sparkled as if it had been hit with an exploding snowball full of light.

Rose felt it like a punch to the stomach.

"*TIE fighters!*" she yelled.

She heard the gasp from across Atterra Bravo's orbit—she was still tuned in to the channel that let her talk to *Treasure*'s flight engineer.

"Oh-one-eight first quadrant high, six of 'em, just like before—"

Meanwhile, Finch flew steadily into the drop zone. The Resistance heavy bombers were committed now, whether or not there were TIE fighters around.

"Cobalt bombers proceed after me—form up behind *Hammer*," Finch ordered. "Lights out, everybody. Fly slow and steady—there's no reason they'll see us unless they come closer."

There was a reason, though—the fact that *Treasure* still showed up on the monitors as a great big power source in the middle of the night sky.

The white sparks disappeared from the screen. Then they swarmed back onto it. It felt like Rose had imaginary lights dancing in front of her eyes.

"Keep an eye on those bandits," Finch warned his crew—which of course was totally unnecessary, as Rose couldn't take her eyes *off* them, and she knew that in their crystal cages suspended in the tail and the foot of the StarFortress, Spennie and Paige were anxiously scanning the skies for the incoming enemy, as well.

And then a terrible thing happened on Rose's screen.

The outline of her own ship began to flicker exactly the way *Treasure*'s had done.

It faded in and out of focus like a poorly tuned hologram.

Rose didn't wait for orders. She scrambled across the flight deck and slid on her back beneath the monstrously awkward piece of equipment that was the power baffler. Rose felt, rather than heard, Spennie's laser cannons firing on the other side of the magnetically sealed shield door next to her head. Again she felt that hollow virtual gut punch of fear. Spennie wouldn't be firing unless they were under attack.

Finch's voice, coming through Rose's headset, was anxious now.

"We've picked up the TIEs."

"We're leaking a power trace. I'm on it," Rose said through her teeth.

"On it!" echoed the tail gunner and Rose's sister, already engaged in battle.

11

ROSE CRAWLED underneath the lower panels of the body of the baffler. This had been so much easier to do wearing nothing but a tank top and work overalls; now she was in a flight suit and rebreather. But she managed to get beneath the awkward piece of equipment and sit up inside it at last.

If I ever do this again, Rose thought, *I will hang this thing in the bomb bay. Or lay it down sideways. There's got to be an easier way.*

The innards of the device automatically lit up when it detected Rose's presence.

"What's your problem?" she demanded. Sometimes it knew.

Her headset translated the series of electronic beeps it gave her in answer: *Synthesizer failure.*

"Nuts and bolts, is that all?"

Rose pulled the synthesizer out of its slot and snapped a new one into place. It took about four seconds to fix.

The baffler beeped a thank-you.

Rose squeezed herself back out from underneath the awkward machine. Almost immediately she collided with the tail gunner, Spennie, who was wheezing and clutching at her rebreather.

"Took a hit—I got one of the fighters, but it exploded close to the ship and a lot of flying debris hit my turret. The turret's solid but the darned *gunsight* shook itself off and came flying at me—it cut one of my air tubes. Take my guns while I seal this thing. You won't be able to aim with accuracy, just blast away at anything you see—"

Spennie broke off, gasping, and sat down to deal with the torn tube.

Rose climbed past her into the gunner's seat in the tail turret.

She didn't even have time to strap herself in before she had to start firing. Through her first volley of random laser blasts, Rose heard Finch call, "Release!"

Seconds later came Nix's response: "Bombs away!"

Rose hoped that the shells, plummeting planetward in the Atterran night, weren't obvious to the enemy attackers.

She couldn't see the shells herself in the dark, and maybe the pilots in the remaining TIEs couldn't see them, either. Maybe no report about the Resistance bomber squadron would make it back to wherever the enemy starfighters were based.

Rose closed off this line of thought and concentrated on the battle. There seemed to be three of the TIEs still throwing themselves in fury at *Hammer*. In the heat of the conflict, Finch suddenly hurled the StarFortress forward in a burst of speed.

The sudden surge made Rose feel for a moment as if she were being yanked in half, as if the great ship were as fragile as a little one-seat landspeeder.

Finch banked sharply. Far below her feet, Rose strained for a glimpse of *Hammer*'s payload of supply canisters. But she couldn't see a thing, and they must have been gone by then.

"I've got Rose's screen," Nix told them all—as soon as the bombs were gone he'd taken over Rose's monitor station.

"Rose has got my guns. And I've got air!" Spennie gasped reassuringly.

I've got a bad feeling about this, thought Rose.

"Hey, Rose," came Paige's calm voice through the headset. "Good to have you up there."

It wasn't good, Rose thought. The TIEs whizzed back and forth across the sky, tacking, and came soaring in for another attack on *Hammer*. Rose blasted at the night randomly, knowing in the pit of her stomach that she didn't have a hope of hitting anything.

It was terrifying. But at least if she and Paige were going to die, they'd die together. . . .

"I can't see *Treasure* anymore," Nix reported from the monitor.

"*Treasure* tech, what's going on?" Rose called anxiously, still connected to the other ship.

There was a moment of crackling interference, and then Cat's voice came through with confidence, "We're out of Bravo's orbit. We're back in the Atterra Belt. Our baffler's fine and we're on course for the hyperspace jump as soon as we clear the asteroid maze."

"We'll miss you," said Rose. *Treasure* was on its own now, and she had other things to worry about.

Without the gunsight, it was impossible to get a decent fix on any of the attacking TIEs. Outside the tail gun turret, Rose could see them whizzing by in the dark like meteors, swarming around the heavy bomber. *Hammer*'s shields were holding against the cannon fire, but they couldn't hold forever.

Paige suddenly gave a whoop that rang in Rose's head, and below her, Rose saw the lower portions of the bomber light briefly with the sunny glow of an explosion.

"*Got you!*" Paige yelled. "*Got you, you arrogant little space spider!*"

"Wow, your competitive streak is showing!" Rose laughed in spite of herself. Paige's usual calm had been shaken.

Did that mean there were only two of the evil things

still flying around out there? Did that mean the Cobalt bomber squadron actually had a chance of winning?

From behind them in the dark, Rose saw a blast of cannon fire slice straight into one of the zooming fighter silhouettes. There was an explosion of radiance in the middle of the night sky. Rose had a perfect view: it was like watching a light show.

Behind *Hammer*, moving forward to its own drop in the dark, the bomber Cobalt *Belle* had taken out one of the TIEs.

Seconds later, another blast came from behind *Belle*— Cobalt *Mare* had also entered the fray.

"Hang in there, kids," Finch called. "I'm powering us down until the rest of the squadron have made their drops. The guns will still be active, but don't fire unless you absolutely have to—I want to use the dark to keep us hidden. The other Forts will cover us. Get ready to wait— we'll be the last to leave."

He paused, and added ominously, "If we last that long, that is."

Rose sat behind her sightless guns in the dark, knowing she'd never be able to target the lone TIE fighter that was swooping around out there. The skin at the back of her neck crawled at the thought that it might fire at her and blow her out of the sky at any moment.

Hammer might survive a direct hit to the tail turret. But Rose wouldn't.

She sat quietly, not firing at the empty sky. She watched *Belle* as it flew in below *Hammer* and emptied its own bomb bays.

Rose wondered where the other TIE fighter was.

The bomber *Mare* followed *Belle* into the drop zone.

"*Belle*, get out of here," Finch commanded. "Don't wait around for the rest of us. If that last TIE escaped . . ."

The pilot let the sentence go unfinished, but Rose thought he was probably thinking exactly what she was thinking.

If the last TIE had retreated—flown back to its base without taking the risk of attacking five armed StarFortress bombers on its own—the pilot of that fighter would without a doubt report the conflict he'd engaged in over Atterra Bravo. And then the First Order would know exactly whom to expect and where to expect them the next time the bombers made the airlift run into Atterra.

It wasn't a pleasant thought.

But at least for now, there was no one shooting at them.

"*Mare* is done," Finch reported from the pilot's cockpit. "Crimson *Dancer* is on the way in, and then there's just Crimson *Bolide* left. After that we'll get out of here. Stay where you are, Rose—Spennie's connected to the main oxygen supply and can't get back to the tail turret. Nix, you've got the tech monitors covered?"

"I'm on it," Nix confirmed.

Rose suddenly remembered that she wasn't strapped in. She wriggled into Spennie's harness and waited for *Dancer* and *Bolide* to make their drops. There was no sign of the last TIE fighter.

The last two bombers sailed away into Atterra Bravo's outer orbit at last, and Finch veered after them and headed toward the Atterra Belt and beyond that the safety of hyperspace.

It didn't seem to take very long. Maybe Finch was getting the hang of navigating the complex system of explosive mines and asteroids. Soon enough came that breathless moment of the jump to lightspeed. Starlight filled the turret and Rose's eyes, then disappeared behind them.

They'd made the drop. The ship was intact. *All the ships* were intact. Nobody was hurt.

From their separate corners of the StarFortress, Rose and the rest of the crew joined voices in a cheer of victory and relief.

They were safe and alone again in the limitless, peaceful mottled blue of hyperspace.

"Get back down here, Rose," Paige said. "Let's ride back to Refnu together."

"How many of those TIE fighters did you actually hit *yourself*?" Rose asked her sister.

Summer on Refnu meant that the dark blue daylight would last late into the evening, but a sleet storm was lashing the docking bays and the Resistance crews could hardly hear each other's shouted greetings. All eleven bombers were safely back in port, and their crews were meeting on foot on the wharf for their mission debriefing—including those ships that had been icebreaking and those that had made the first airlift run to Atterra.

"I got three of 'em. And I'm not even flying a fighter ship!" Paige caught her breath. She didn't do a lot of boasting. But she was obviously pleased with herself.

"*Three TIE fighters!*" Rose repeated. "Wow—should I start calling you Master Paige? Are you a Jedi or something?"

Rose only half meant it as a joke. She was in awe of Paige's gunnery skill—and, really, of every other skill her older sister possessed.

Paige laughed at Rose's teasing.

"When they're flying straight at you, it's not hard to see them."

It had been hard to aim at them, though, Rose remembered with a shiver. Of course Paige had had a working gunsight, but still . . .

"Bet it makes you wish you were flying a starfighter," Rose said.

"I never even think about that when I'm shooting!" Paige said. "But you know what? It explains why I get so frustrated when they fly out of range. I can't fly after them."

"You know what that means . . ." Rose reminded her. "One of them got away."

Paige turned to Rose and stared at her, alarmed and frowning. "Are we sure about that?"

"No one can confirm shooting it," Rose said. "Maybe that TIE pilot doesn't know how many of us there were. But he's going to make a report, for sure."

It was a sobering thought.

Fossil had come along to Refnu to manage her squadrons. Casca Panzoro was with her, anxious to hear how the first rescue mission to her homeworld had gone. Casca and Fossil, along with the bomber unit's flight surgeon, Tiggs Kaiga, met with the StarFortress crews on the wharf.

When they'd begun to gather, Fossil pointed at the supply transport that had come with the squadrons. Five dozen or so bomber crew members plus ground personnel made their way through the service hatch and gathered on the loading floor of the transport, where there were portable heaters set up.

"The rumor is that the first Atterra run turned into quite the adventure," quipped Fossil. "Tiggs is delighted you've brought yourselves back with no more damage than a sound night's sleep will easily repair."

Everyone murmured "Of course," "Yes," "No problem." The StarFortress squadron teams adored their Old Lady, despite her terrifying appearance. She managed to make every single one of them feel indispensable.

"Casca Panzoro has a few words with which she would like to grace you," said Fossil.

The district representative of the Firestone Islands gave Fossil a sober, grateful glance, and stood straight before the gathered assembly.

"Thank you," said Casca Panzoro. *"Thank you."* The gratitude in her voice, and on her face, was warm and full of relief. It made her look younger. "Even if the rest of this mission doesn't go as planned, *thank you* for beginning it. Thank you for believing in us. Thank you for your lives, your gifts, your generosity—but most of all, your *trust.*"

Casca paused, and added in a low voice, "May the Force be with you."

There was an awkward little moment's silence, and then the bomber crews broke into spontaneous applause.

After a few moments Fossil quieted them down by lifting her large hand.

"Well spoken, Casca," she said, and Casca moved aside to let Fossil take control of the assembly again.

Fossil set to business straightaway.

"I will be pleased if the baffler technicians can give me full reports on what went wrong," she told them. "Afterward I will be following the maintenance teams as we make ready for tomorrow's shipment. There is ample fuel for all ships tomorrow, and the next day, but for our final mission the transport must return for fuel to—"

Fossil paused, and rumbled as if she were clearing her throat. There was to be no mention of D'Qar on this assignment, just in case someone might be listening.

"To the main depot," she finished blandly. "First, let us discuss today's events."

———

The summer sleet storm was in full howl when Fossil dismissed everybody. Now Rose had to go along with each of the flight engineers to check that all was in place for the next day's bombing run. She was grateful no one from Refnu seemed to guess that eleven of the five dozen ships moored there had a secret purpose that had nothing to do with excavating ore from the surface of an isolated world.

Before Rose did anything else, though, she went along with Cat to make sure he'd rewired all of *Treasure*'s baffler plugs correctly.

The Refnu native was a hulking young man so big-boned and bulky that he towered two full heads taller than Rose, and she was surprised to find him huddling against her and hanging on to her elbow as they battled the wind.

Rose wasn't very big—she couldn't have been much support in the storm's deep dusk while they crossed the docks. As they entered the bay where the heavy bomber *Treasure* loomed, its massive height swaying slightly in the wind as if it couldn't wait to take off again, Cat ducked his head and shouted into the storm, making an excuse for himself.

"I hate being outside," he said, turning sheepishly away from Rose but still hanging on to her arm. "I'd rather be sitting in a bomber that's going up in flames than standing out here in the wind."

"Are you kidding? You grew up here on Refnu!"

He shook his head, huddling in the shelter of the bomber *Treasure* while Rose got the hatch open at the bottom of the empty clip that hadn't been replaced yet.

"I grew up *inside*. We never went out if we could help it. I don't mind flying in a storm, but I don't like being *out* in it."

Rose let Cat climb into the bomber first, and she let him sit down for a moment to catch his breath while she powered up the ground-based light and heat systems. They couldn't get up the ladder past the bomb racks in their bulky outdoor gear, and it would take a minute or so for the interior of the StarFortress to warm up enough for them to take off their parkas.

"Wow," Rose said, waiting with him. "I guess you usually use the tunnels to get around."

"I sure do."

Cat glanced up at her and said in a low voice, "I'll tell you a secret. When I'm on a bombing run, and we're skimming the surface of some inner planet—when it's day, and there aren't any clouds, and all you can see above you is blue sky and it's so bright you have to wear filters—I pray to every atom in the galaxy that I won't ever have to stand outside, unprotected, and look up at an empty sky like that. All that space. It scares me so bad it makes me sick. I don't even like being in the cockpits when we're flying. Darn right I grew up on Refnu. We don't have windows here. I like to see *walls*."

Listening to Cat talk, Rose grew suddenly aware of the smooth pendant lying against her skin beneath the layers of protective clothing—the piece of ore from the Otomok system that her parents had given her, the piece of home she shared with her sister—a hard keepsake from a cold, dark world bound with ice clouds.

Like Cat, Rose had grown up on an icebound planet where the living quarters never had windows, and people worked underground or on board insulated ships.

Rose loved her destroyed home fiercely.

But she wasn't like Cat at all. She *longed* to stand outside, unprotected, and look up at a bright and empty sky.

She thought about it while she and Cat counted circuit sequences, and she couldn't understand it at all.

12

FOSSIL WAS waiting for them when they descended to ground level again.

"All well?" Fossil rumbled. "I know what a responsibility this is for you, Rose Tico."

"It's all good," said Rose, not sure she meant it but knowing that it was what Fossil wanted to hear. She didn't think Fossil realized how much the responsibility scared her. "We had trouble with *Treasure*'s power baffler on this run, but Cat knew exactly what to do."

"I have a request for you, Rose Tico," said Fossil. "*Wasp*'s flight engineer is struggling to adjust to the climate here on Refnu. She returned sick and shaking after the journey to the ice mines today, and Tiggs wants her to rest for a day under the sunlamps before she flies again. If your bombardier, Nix, were to cover your monitors, could you fly with *Wasp* on tomorrow's mission to Atterra in place of their technician?"

Rose nearly said yes. It was such a simple, reasonable request.

But something inside her began to unravel a little and stopped her from answering right away.

Then, when she did answer, Rose found herself trying to make an excuse.

"Leave Nix on his own with the baffler? No way. He doesn't understand the little monster."

"I am surprised," Fossil commented. "You are usually one who obeys commands, yet now, when called upon for support, you criticize another's skill. You have trained the other flight engineers. You can train your bombardier. You know this. What is your real objection?"

Rose knew that the truth had nothing to do with obeying commands.

She hesitated, then admitted softly, "I've never flown without my sister."

She didn't think she *could* fly without Paige.

Cat stood listening, hanging back a step or two without interrupting, a little embarrassed.

"You have always before accommodated my requests," Fossil said. She seemed curious rather than angry. "You have never refused."

Aware of Cat listening, Rose flailed to make herself sound less cowardly. "I'm like one of those sonar swallows. I can only fly as one of a pair." *Ugh,* she thought, *that doesn't sound funny—just super sentimental.* Rose added unhappily, "I *know* I'm the tech support for the power bafflers. But I just don't want to fly without Paige."

Rose thought of Reeve Panzoro, and of how he'd accused her of never being able to make a decision without getting Paige's okay.

But Rose knew this was different. This had nothing to do with what Paige thought.

The fear that Rose scrunched into a ball in a corner of her brain while she was focused on an operational bombing run—while she was climbing from the bomb bay to the tech monitors, scrambling around in the innards of the baffler, or emerging to take over the damaged guns of the tail turret—that fear stayed put because Rose *knew* Paige was down there in calm control of the laser cannons beneath the bomb bays.

She knew that Paige was down there, waiting for Rose to join her again when the danger was past.

See you then, Rose.

It wasn't a question of decision making. Rose couldn't *imagine* flight without Paige.

"This is an awkward time to demonstrate lack of moral fiber," Fossil told Rose coolly. "It is the day before a mission in which you are a vital component."

"I know. I'm *sorry.* Paige doesn't know," Rose apologized. "Couldn't you swap her around, too, so we could fly together? You said when we joined the Resistance that you'd always let us fly in the same crew."

Fossil gazed down at Rose with unreadable wide crystalline silver eyes, bemused.

Cat said suddenly, "I'll go."

Rose and Fossil both turned to look at him. Cat gave Rose a smile. She remembered how he'd confessed his secret fear to her, his fear of being outside. He understood fear.

"Sure, I'll go," Cat repeated. "Why not? I made a mistake today I'm not likely to make again. I know the circuit sequences for the power bafflers by heart now. I don't need to adjust to the climate at all—this is my home. I'll go with *Wasp* as their technician, and Rose can stay with her own crew."

Rose and Cat looked to Fossil for approval. Their commander shrugged.

"Your cooperation as a unit, as always, moves and pleases me," she said in her rumbling voice.

She hadn't said yes yet, though. Rose bit her lip, waiting for the final decision.

The Old Lady nodded. "Sonar swallows indeed. No one has used *that* as an excuse before."

"Thank you," Rose breathed. "Thank you, Fossil. *Thank you*, Cat."

"What a goof you are, Rose," Paige told her fondly as they sat squeezed tight together in the lower gun turret during the next day's hyperspace journey to Atterra for the second airlift bombing run. "Cute, but a goof."

"Shut up." Rose felt self-conscious about her stubborn and childish insistence on flying with her big sister. Fossil hadn't mentioned the request to the other crew members, but Cat had said something to Paige about Rose's "sisterly devotion," and Rose didn't want to talk about it.

Paige heard the tone of Rose's voice, though, and she got it. She apologized.

"You know I'm teasing. I'm a little jealous of how indispensable you are to this mission."

"You're jealous of *me*?" said Rose, who felt that she would never be as multitalented, as calm, or as respected as her older sister. "Did you hit your head on one of those Atterra asteroids?"

"I'm totally serious!" Paige assured her. "Everyone's a little scared of those bafflers. And it's not because they don't trust them—it's because they're so impressed that you managed to scrape together such a complicated piece of equipment in such a short time. I was talking to *Cutter* and *Hornet*'s technicians about it in the cafeteria last night. They're all worried they'll make some dumb mistake like Cat did, and just knowing you're there to talk to them makes them feel reassured. They're very glad you're here."

It was Rose's turn to tease. "You're always gossiping."

But she felt warm inside, and a little sick with the awful responsibility of being in charge of them all.

"Got to get up to the flight deck for our return to real-space," Rose added. "See you on the way back to Refnu."

Paige was calm as always. "See you then, Rose," she answered.

————

Four Cobalt Squadron heavy bombers, with two Crimson Squadron bombers supporting them, began to emerge from hyperspace on the outside of the Atterra Belt.

It was quiet there. The complex space ahead of them loomed ominously, but the outer planetary orbit of the Atterra system seemed wholly empty. It was as peaceful as the limitless mottled blue of hyperspace.

Rose, watching the monitors, saw the shape of Crimson *Cutter* first; then Cobalt *Wasp* and *Scarab* appeared on the screen, their unwieldy familiar bulky outlines reassuring. *Hammer* entered the asteroid maze just after Cobalt *Hornet* and Crimson *Hailstorm* emerged from hyperspace. As soon as the asteroids of the Atterra Belt blocked the other bombers from *Hammer*'s line of sight, they winked off the monitors. The power bafflers were all working.

The bombers were on their own as they navigated the

Atterra Belt—they'd regroup on the other side to enter Atterra Bravo's orbit in formation.

The Resistance bombers couldn't see each other as they flew through the Atterra Belt, but they could talk to each other, and with each trip, they mapped more booby traps. They were beginning to be able to guess the size and nature of the asteroids likely to hide an automatic cannon. They were also getting better at gauging the perfect distance for avoiding laser fire while still being able to use the asteroids to hide behind.

But Rose's heart was hammering in her chest as they made their way between the asteroids. She was expecting an attack the whole way in; that one escaped TIE yesterday had *surely* reported them.

But there was nothing. The belt was quiet.

The attack came as they flew toward Atterra Bravo on the other side of the belt.

Hammer took the initial fury of the enemy fire. Seconds after they emerged from the cover of the Atterra Belt, a squadron of TIE fighters came streaking straight after them.

With the attack coming from behind, the bomber *Hammer* was lucky enough to be between the TIEs and the sun, and Finch immediately veered to take advantage of having the light at their back. He unleashed a blaze of laser fire from the forward cannons.

As the clutch of TIEs shot back, *Hammer*'s shields held. The six TIEs went screaming away toward Atterra Bravo's night before wheeling in for another attack. But now Spennie and Paige, in their rearward-facing gun turrets, were able to get a good shot at them.

Hammer met the second attack with furious gunfire.

Rose was in agony, though. Nix was remotely controlling the cannons in the dorsal turret from the bombardier's computer pedestal. But there was absolutely nothing Rose herself could do to help the fight. She looked out over the pilot's shoulder, trying not to get in Finch's way. She could feel the ship shuddering as the TIEs fired on them from behind. Finch was tense, waiting for the attack to move around to the front. A split second later he was firing like fury again.

Rose backed away into the windowless bulk of the fuselage. There was something suffocating about being able to see this attack without being able to fire back. It was worse than sitting in a gunner's turret under fire herself.

Then it occurred to Rose that there *was* something she could do: she could warn the other bombers so that they wouldn't be taken by surprise when they came out of the protective camouflage of the Atterra Belt.

Rose hit the general comm button fixed to her headset, the feature she now shared with the pilot so that she'd be able to talk to the technicians in the other bombers without having to be patched in.

"There are TIE fighters inside the belt!" she yelled. "Alert your crew!"

Crimson *Cutter*'s flight engineer reported from his station, where Rose knew he must have his eyes glued to the monitors.

"I see them. Wasp is covering us. We're coming to help you."

Another handful of white lights appeared on Rose's monitor. Her heart sank.

"Wasp *and* Cutter, *defend yourselves, not us!*" Rose cried. "Scarab, Hornet, Hailstorm—*tell your gunners to look sharp!*" She didn't even think about the fact that she was shouting commands at flight crews she had no business being in charge of. It never occurred to her she had no authority to tell them how to fly their mission. She was just trying desperately to warn them, to save them from disaster.

From the lower gun turret, Paige had seen the new clutch of TIEs, and called in a frantic warning cry for the rest of *Cutter*'s crew.

"Bandits! Bandits! Beware, Cutter! *TIE fighters on Crimson* Cutter! *Somebody tell 'em—there's another clutch of TIEs coming for* Cutter!"

The *Cutter* technician's voice then came through sounding just as frantic, and Rose, staring at her own monitor, knew why.

"I see four more squadrons inbound!" he cried. "The first must have sounded an alert when they found us, and called for reinforcements—"

The monitor screens were dazzling with white sparks. They came in clustered handfuls from three directions at once, in addition to the individual fighters that were already focused on *Hammer*. The StarFortress shook with the impact of the shots against the blast shields, with the action of the gunners firing back, and with the movement of Finch's evasive weaving.

With swift and purposeful calculation, one of the approaching squadrons of fighters swarmed toward the incoming bomber *Wasp*. Another squadron went after *Scarab*. The third and fourth approaching squadron of TIEs held back—they were waiting for *Hornet* and *Hailstorm*. There was a whole squadron of TIE fighters ready to take on every one of the Resistance bombers.

Another squadron arrived as Rose watched the screen.

The bomber *Hammer* somehow continued to hold its own. Rose's screen swarmed so thickly with the white traces of the TIEs that she couldn't tell how many of them *Hammer*'s guns had managed to defeat. She thought that the shocks coming at the ship were not as frequent as they'd been. Unformed bolts of hope stabbed through her head: *Last time we were okay—maybe if we just get the ones after us, maybe we can get through this first attack—*

That was when *Wasp's* trace on the technical monitor suddenly vanished.

There was no great burst of noise to announce the moment, no deafening roar of the blast that obliterated the ship as there would have been if it had happened inside a planet's atmosphere. There was a dull crackle of static as *Wasp's* comms went blank, and then silence in the space where the ship had been.

At the same time, Paige and Spennie gave simultaneous wordless cries of anguish. They'd seen the explosion.

The TIEs that had been surrounding *Wasp* swooped away, splitting off into twos, and each pair joined one of the squadrons attacking the remaining bombers.

For a few moments Rose's brain refused to believe it. Then: *We've lost an entire ship.*

Cat's ship. What had he said to her the night before?

I hate being outside. I'd rather be sitting in a bomber that's going up in flames than standing out here in the wind.

She thought of his tall, bulky Refnian body crammed inside *Wasp's* baffler, frantically struggling with the plugs—but no, there hadn't been anything wrong with *Wasp's* baffler. Cat would have been staring at the tech screens just as Rose was now, watching the storm of white sparks that were the TIE fighters dancing in and out among the slower shapes of the Resistance StarFortresses.

Had the ship exploded so suddenly that Cat didn't know what was happening? One minute feeling secure in an enclosed space, and the next . . . ?

He'd flown in her place.

Fossil had asked Rose to fly on *Wasp*, and Cat had taken her place.

Rose knew she couldn't think about it—not now. She'd lost people before—crew members and family both. In the middle of a battle she couldn't think about it.

In the middle of a battle there were other things to think about.

Three dozen TIE fighters.

How many of that first squadron were still pursuing *Hammer*—joined now by two of the clutch that had blasted *Wasp* out of the sky? There were eight of the ferocious sparks drilling into *Scarab's* outline on the screen now—

"Finch," Rose begged over the internal comm to *Hammer's* pilot, "we should abort the mission."

She gulped in another breath, and hurried on: "We should turn back *now*. We can't keep up a battle like this all the way to Bravo's surface, and if we *do*, we'll give away the position of our scheduled drops—you've got to give the command!"

"I was going to anyway," Finch gasped. "Just waiting for someone else to suggest it. . . ."

But he was too busy defending his own ship to give the order right away. Firing back at the attackers, he veered suddenly planetward.

"You're heading into the minefield!" Paige yelled.

"I know—"

The StarFortress couldn't make a tight turn, but Finch suddenly threw on full power and soared in a different direction. Three of the TIEs, overenthusiastic in their pursuit and knowing they had superior maneuverability, flew straight into the minefield and exploded within seconds.

The pilot didn't waste a moment on triumph.

"Cobalt Squadron, Crimson support, retreat," Finch yelled as the other starfighters careened out of his reach for a moment. *"All bombers retreat.* Don't wait—"

The command came too late.

Hornet had already emerged behind *Scarab*. One of the unoccupied squadrons of TIEs was ready for it. They came leaping out of their holding pattern to attack.

They were picking off the Resistance heavy bombers like beads off a string—just waiting for them to appear and shooting them out of the sky as easily and predictably as a line of gaming targets.

Finch had given the order to retreat, but he hadn't

shown any inclination to move *Hammer* out of the line of fire.

"You getting out or not?" Nix called to *Hammer*'s pilot.

The bombardier got no response at first. As before, Finch was firing at one of the approaching starfighters as it screamed back for another deadly, swooping pass. The explosion, when Finch hit the TIE, was close enough that for half a second it floodlit the entire interior of the bomber's fuselage with a deep and flickering golden glow.

"Got to see it through for the rest of 'em, I think," Finch grunted. "I'm trying to stay close to *Cutter* so we can give them some cover. . . .

"We're responsible," he added, as he guided the StarFortress to dive away through the cloud of gleaming cinders that was all that was left of the TIE fighter he'd just destroyed. "Don'tcha think? You with me?"

"Sure we are," sighed Nix.

"Here," confirmed Paige briefly from the lower gun turret, and Spennie echoed, "Here."

Rose answered with more gloom than usual: "Ready for anything."

Finch began, "Because I think—"

He didn't finish his sentence. His words were cut off as the last of *Scarab*'s shields fell and the surrounding enemy starfighters moved in on the defenseless StarFortress to finish the job.

The dreadful thing about *Scarab*'s destruction was that Rose and Finch, tuned in to common frequencies so they could communicate with the rest of the Resistance bombers, could hear the crew's screams as the ship burned.

For a terrible thirty seconds, in a fit of panic, Rose switched off her headset so she didn't have to listen.

It was the longest thirty seconds of her life.

When there was nothing left on the screen where *Scarab*'s outline had been, Rose flipped her headset's power back on.

Finch was shouting: *"Retreat! Retreat! RETREAT!"*

13

CUTTER HAD disappeared from Rose's screen. She didn't know if it was because they'd also been destroyed, or because they'd made it back into the shelter of the Atterra Belt and the line of sight was broken.

"Crimson *Cutter*!" she called. "*Cutter* tech, can you hear me?"

There was no answer.

Hailstorm, the last of the heavy bombers to emerge from the maze of asteroids, had already changed direction. The TIEs that had lain in wait for it were streaking toward it but hadn't reached it yet, and *Hailstorm* was traveling at top speed back toward the belt. Rose's heart vaulted with a sudden overdose of hope and gladness—the adrenaline rush lasted about half a second, and then she stopped watching, because *Hailstorm* wasn't her concern anymore. Nor was *Cutter* or *Wasp* or *Scarab*. Besides *Hammer* itself, there was only *Hornet* left.

On the monitors, *Hornet* made a wide loop. Like *Hammer*, it didn't have a very tight turning circle. The remaining TIE fighters whizzed back and forth around it like a flock of sonar swallows mobbing someone who stood singing at the top of her voice in the D'Qar forest— except the birds of D'Qar didn't deliver deadly blasts of laser fire as they came flying close.

Rose saw a few of the dazzling enemy images go dark as the Resistance gunners managed to destroy some of the TIE fighters.

But there were too many for the heavy bombers to destroy them all. Their only hope now lay in escape.

The bomber *Hornet* finished making its turn, and Finch put on a burst of speed to try to fly close behind the other StarFortress.

"Safety in numbers—" Finch panted. "If any of those bandits come between us we'll get them—aw, *for the love of a loaded stun gun.*"

He broke off, cursing, as something solid hit the top of the cockpit.

"Are the shields holding?" Spennie asked anxiously from the tail turret.

"Just about," Finch grunted, concentrating on flight.

Rose could see the problem on the monitors. Pieces of the destroyed bombers were getting in their path. "The sky's full of debris," she told the crew. "But that's not a bad thing—it's helping us. . . ."

"Yeah, I saw a TIE collide with a chunk of scrap metal a second ago," Paige confirmed.

"Those TIEs are going so fast they can't get out of the way," said Finch. "We're big enough it doesn't hurt us, but what a mess—"

He broke off suddenly and said in quiet defeat, "They got *Hornet*."

―――――――

Hammer flew through the explosion. It helped keep the TIE fighters away from the bomber as *Hammer* made its lonely escape back through the asteroids and then, finally, to the quiet blue safety of hyperspace.

―――――――

When the bomber *Hammer* entered realspace just beyond Refnu, Rose was relieved to see that *Hailstorm's* familiar shape was moving steadily ahead of them.

Three Cobalt Squadron ships were never coming back, and there was no sign of the other Crimson bomber.

No one spoke more than was required as they went through the landing sequence. The *Hammer* crew didn't even speak to each other after they'd docked and were struggling into their weathersuits. Paige reached out to squeeze Rose's hand; that was it.

At last Finch said, "We're to report to the Old Lady for debriefing in common room twenty-three in the harbormaster's complex. She called in while I was docking. That Bravo Rising resistance leader will be there, too. *Hailstorm*'s crew is all right."

Miraculously, no one on board *Hammer* had been hurt, either.

They tumbled into the debriefing room and struggled out of their weathersuits again. For a moment all was chaos as the two surviving crews rushed into one another's arms. The room Fossil had managed to set aside for them was much too big for the twelve people gathered there—Fossil had been expecting to accommodate more than thirty.

Hailstorm's pilot and Spennie began to sob. Everyone else was silent.

"Please sit. Get warm." There were blankets and protein portions and hot drinks; Fossil pointed. "We have a surprise for you."

Casca Panzoro was presiding over a very ancient portable organic synthicator, which shuddered with the effort of producing something edible out of a mixture of powdered starches. After a moment Fossil crossed over to it and opened the production drawer, rolled back the lid, and with delicate, enormous fingers, flicked away a layer of styrochips. Beneath the protective chips lay four round fruits about the size of Rose's fist. They were the flaming color of a D'Qar sunset.

"Starberries?" breathed *Hailstorm*'s pilot. "Where on this winter planet . . . ?"

"It is no tree-grown fruit," Fossil explained. "Nothing real. They are synthicated clones. The image of starberries—as the inhabitants of Refnu live beneath the image of sunlight within their windowless walls."

Rose had never seen such a thing. She stared, along with every other crew member of the returning heavy bombers.

"It's synthetic, but it's still fresh fruit," Casca said. "It won't last two of this planet's long days. You're working and dying for *us*—for a pair of distant worlds that most of you have never set foot on." She looked up, with the fleeting warm glance that made her seem younger. "You're not expecting any payment. As far as I can tell, your sacrifice is for nothing other than the satisfaction of being able to fight for what you believe in."

"Take this fruit and eat it in memory of your fallen comrades," Fossil said. She pulled the drawer free of the synthicator and held it forward.

"Pilots and flight engineers first," she added. "We will make a second and third small harvest for the gunners and bombardiers, and I will hear your report while we wait."

Fossil, Casca, and the gunners and bombardiers of both ships watched solemnly while the pilots and technicians ate the rosy synthicated fruit.

Rose looked around her as she nibbled at the astonishingly crisp, sweet flesh. It seemed utterly unreal after the harsh brutality of the last Atterra run, and she could tell that Finch and the *Hailstorm* crew members felt the same way. Their faces were as drained and passionless as if they were eating dust. They were forcing it down as a ritual— *in memory of your fallen comrades.*

"Tell me how it began," Fossil said.

Haltingly, and with many corrections and interruptions, the *Hailstorm* and *Hammer* crews began to tell the story of the day's failed mission.

By the time they'd finished, Casca had created two more batches of starberries for the rest of the StarFortress crews. Fossil passed the fruit around without speaking except to prompt the pilots or gunners to continue their tale. But when they'd exhausted what they had to say, and *Hailstorm*'s pilot started to cry again, Fossil gave her throat-clearing rumble and began to ask unsettling and probing questions.

"Describe again what you saw on the screen, Rose Tico, as you watched *Hailstorm* flying from the carnage. How was it that the bomber *Hailstorm* managed to escape the fate of the others?"

"They were—they were the last in the line. They were able to turn around in time. By the time the—the enemy squadron got close to them, they were already back in the asteroid belt and—and I guess . . ."

Rose hesitated, because she didn't actually know what had happened after that.

Hailstorm's pilot shrugged. He rubbed his eyes, gave one last sob, and spoke steadily.

He said, "We got lucky. Two of the fighters on our tail collided with one of the asteroids, and we lost the others for a little while, and we were ready for the lightspeed jump the second we were out of the asteroid belt. We couldn't have done it without the shields, or the power baffler, or the gunners."

The pilot glanced over at his own gunners, both fur-covered humanoids. They were seated side by side with arms clasped over each other's shoulders. *Hailstorm*'s pilot and gunners exchanged a quiet moment, communicating only with their eyes.

"Mainly we couldn't have done it without the gunners," *Hailstorm*'s pilot amended. "But we couldn't have done it without the command to retreat, either, or if we hadn't been the farthest back in the line."

"Ah." Fossil turned back to Finch and his crew. "The order in the lineup mattered. I would like to hear, then, *Hammer* crew: You were first in line. You were first out, first fired on, and last to leave. What is the reason you believe you were spared?"

Rose and her crewmates all stared at each other in bewilderment.

Until this moment, it hadn't occurred to them that there might be any reason other than the ones the *Hailstorm* pilot had just mentioned, plus Finch's own ability as a pilot: good luck, the shields, the power baffler, and Paige and Spennie's accuracy when firing the laser cannons.

But they'd been under fire for longer, and with more of the TIEs on top of them, than any of the other heavy bombers.

"I guess maybe they let us go," Finch said slowly.

Rose saw Paige nodding.

"They might have wanted a ship they could trace," Paige guessed. "They might have wanted to follow us back to wherever we came from. . . ."

"They might have suspected you of coming from a base on Atterra Alpha, perhaps, and wanted to track you there," suggested Casca Panzoro. "Or even from one of the asteroids in the Atterra Belt. Some of them have settlements. And because you got away through hyperspace, they'll know now that you're coming from outside the system."

"We shall check the hulls," rumbled Fossil. "They may

have successfully planted a tracking device during the battle. We will take no risks. Yes, Nix?"

"They might have wanted to take prisoners," *Hammer's* bombardier croaked, as if it had just occurred to him. "If they'd disabled us enough to board us, or to hold us until another ship arrived, they could have . . . they could have tried to question us, or . . ."

He finished raggedly, "We know a *lot*."

"I trust you would have had the sense to destroy yourselves before such a thing happened," Fossil said drily.

Rose and Finch nodded in agreement so quickly that Fossil never even had a chance to doubt their resolve.

Rose would *never* let herself be taken prisoner by *anyone* in the First Order. If she had to blow herself and her sister up together, she'd do it.

She exchanged a piercing glance with Paige and knew that her sister felt the same way. Rose felt even more certain about it now than she'd felt before the day's disastrous events.

"So," Fossil concluded. "The TIE that escaped on your first trip reported back to the First Order patrol masters in Atterra Alpha, who saw to it that an ambush was lying in wait for you on your second trip. We have failed to make our second drop. We have lost nearly an entire airlift supply shipment, along with four bombers and their associated crew. We have little time to spare. But we will not fly to Atterra tomorrow. We need to repair our spirits and consider a new strategy before we risk ourselves in another suicidal mission."

Fossil turned away from the two remaining crews, and Rose suddenly realized that the overbearing, authoritative unit commander was as broken with grief and loss as her own crews were.

"We will speak again tomorrow," the Old Lady said quietly. "And then we shall move forward."

Her large, shining silver hand caught the artificial light as she dismissed them.

In the middle of the night Rose was woken from a fitful, fire-filled sleep by Paige stroking her face and saying her name over and over.

"Rose, Rose! Wake up—good news—"

Rose sat up instantly, banging her head on the top of the sleeping bay. She was on the upper level and there wasn't room to sit up there. Below her, where Paige stood, the soft blue light they were allowed to game or chat by during quiet hours was illuminating Paige's bunk.

"Come down, come join us, Rose—"

Rose rolled over and swung down by Paige's side.

There, sitting on Paige's bunk, was their friend Vennie, who'd flown as the pilot for the bomber *Cutter.*

Rose actually rubbed her eyes. *"What—how in the name of all galaxies—"*

"Cutter came back," Paige explained simply, her eyes shining.

Rose leaped at Vennie and hugged her spontaneously. Like Paige, Vennie was a multitalented pilot. She sometimes flew an A-wing, going along as an escort for the bombers. But now, since there was no fighter escort for them, she was doubling as a StarFortress pilot.

Paige drew Rose down next to her so that all three of them were sitting tight together in the low blue light of Paige's bunk, Paige squeezed in between Rose and Vennie. Paige curled one protective and comforting arm fondly around each of their backs on either side of her.

"Our hyperdrive was damaged in the fight," explained Vennie. "We made it out of the Atterra system, but stalled out of lightspeed in some backwater on the Outer Rim— we couldn't even find a place to land, just sat orbiting some worldless star for a while. We spent twelve hours floating there, regenerating power and tying the ship back together. That's why it took us so long. I don't know how you techs do it, to tell the truth—ours managed to fix the hyperdrive with parts from your power baffler. . . ."

"No way!" Rose couldn't help laughing.

"You'll have to ask our tech what he did. Actually, someone's bound to talk to you about it, because he had to break up the power baffler to get the hyperdrive to work, and you'll have to rebuild it."

"I will totally do that without complaining," Rose vowed, "since it got you back here somehow."

"Well, that's what we do best, isn't it?" said Paige. "Work together without complaining."

Rose rolled her eyes. "I complain."

"You're the little sister. You're allowed to complain."

"I wouldn't, if you weren't so bossy," Rose teased.

Paige and Vennie both laughed. It felt *good* to tease a little. It felt good to have something to be glad about.

Vennie said, "I came straight to the Tico sisters after we docked—because we wouldn't be here without you. *Thank you both* for saving our lives. We'd never have managed to bum our way out of Atterra without being seen if it hadn't been for that power baffler, and we'd never even have gotten that far if it hadn't been for *Hammer* covering us with your guns when those starfighters first attacked us."

Vennie faltered, her voice shaking with emotion. Despite the joy of their reunion, none of them had recovered from the stunning shock of what had happened to the Cobalt Squadron.

"You're so right, Paige," Vennie finished, with feeling. "Working together—it's what we do best. Our ships, *Hammer* and *Cutter*, we were the first two in—those starfighters should have easily beaten us both, or one of us anyway. But you protected us. You gave us the chance we needed to escape."

Paige didn't answer right away, but Rose felt her sister's arm tightening around her waist, and she knew that Paige had something on her mind—something that had struck her very suddenly.

"What's up?" Rose asked quietly.

"It was what you said about how we worked together, Vennie," Paige said slowly. "You said our cover gave you the chance to escape."

"I guess you just did what a fighter escort would have done," Vennie said. "You did what I'd have done if I'd been flying a starfighter. But of course I'm not flying a starfighter. And we don't have a fighter escort, and we're not going to get one, either."

"But we could protect each *other*," said Paige. "I mean, obviously we do that anyway. But maybe we could use a little strategy and do it *better*. Maybe we could do it aggressively—*on purpose*."

"How do you mean?" Vennie asked, intrigued.

Rose had seen the wheels turning like this in Paige's mind before. Paige's ability to seize on a little thing and turn it into a strategic plan was what had gotten them out of the Otomok system alive.

"Here's the thing," said Paige. "Today we entered Atterra Bravo's orbit in an orderly parade, predictable as planets lining up around a star. So one way we could avoid the enemy picking us off in line is to split up—not fly as a squadron. Everyone approach the target from a different position."

"Um, that's a little suicidal," Rose pointed out. "Doesn't it leave the Forts without *any* protection?"

"Yeah, but what if we went in pairs? Fossil thinks they purposefully let our ship go because they were hoping to track it. What if we went in pairs, with the first ship going in as a kind of decoy, to draw the attention away from the other? The very first ship could be empty—then it would be faster and more maneuverable, and it could distract the TIEs while the second ship made a drop—maybe on the other side of the planet. Then—"

As often happened when Paige got an idea, Rose saw where she was going with it.

"Then the first ship could escape," Rose interrupted, "and the second, which would be empty once its supplies were dropped, could act as a decoy for the next that came in!"

"We'd have to time it and plot the coordinates pretty carefully," said Vennie. "But I see! This way there would be only two ships in Atterra Bravo's orbit at any one time, so we'd all be at less of a risk—"

"And if we came in from different entry points, they wouldn't be able to pick us off like they did today," finished Paige breathlessly.

"That's a *desperate* plan, Paige Tico," Rose told her sister.

"But?"

The three survivors of that day's disastrous Atterra run grinned at one another like conspirators.

"But it just might work, right?" said Paige.

Vennie stood up and stretched. "I'm heading to my bunk," she said. "That was the longest day I've ever spent on the Outer Rim. Got to get some rest if we're going to get these ships packed and repaired for tomorrow."

"We get tomorrow off," said Rose.

"That was last night," Paige reminded her. "We've only got today off. Tomorrow we're back out there."

14

*T*WO MORE DROPS, Rose told herself throughout the day whenever she had time to worry about the future. *Or—no, I guess we need to make three more. Because we didn't actually make one yesterday. Only three more drops and then we can go back to D'Qar.*

Their "day off" wasn't by any means a vacation. All the remaining bomb rack clips and supplies had to be shifted out of the transport; the empty clips had to be loaded back into it so the transport could return to D'Qar for fuel for the final airlifts. There were repairs to be made. There were still six ships scheduled to make the Atterra run the next day, but that left only two to make the icebreaking run, which they had to continue if they wanted to maintain their cover on Refnu.

———

Sometimes Rose felt that the toughest part of a bombing run was the time they spent stuck in the ship doing nothing: the dead time of *waiting*. All that bottled-up grief and fear and energy and preparation, and there they were sitting doing *nothing*.

They were ready to go the following morning, but a howling storm was preventing any of the bombers from taking off. The storm was predicted to pass in a couple of hours; there wasn't any point in leaving the ship and waiting somewhere else.

Hammer's crew sat on the floor of the flight deck playing sabacc with a deck of very worn cards that Finch kept strapped beneath the pilot's seat just in case they found themselves with time on their hands. Playing cards was a small way to pretend there was nothing wrong with their nerves.

Without anything of value to wager, they usually bet on imaginary racing beasts. In the game, they each owned a stable housing six sleek fathiers—Paige's idea, of course. No one in *Hammer*'s crew had ever seen a real one. These long-legged, elegant land creatures ran in swift, wild herds on brighter, more central planets, where the elite of the galaxy rode them mounted as racers and hunters.

"No way, I'm not risking my silver mare," Paige told Finch. "Not with *these* cards."

The bombardier, Nix, gave a snort. "Well, I'll bet my bronze mare, then—how about you, Rose?"

Rose slapped down her cards in frustration. The

waiting felt worse than usual and the pretended distraction wasn't working. "You can have my whole herd. *Nuts and bolts*, the wind has *stopped*. What is taking the Old Lady so long with that clearance?"

Finch was edgy, too. At Rose's outburst he stood up and went to peer out into the twilight darkness of Refnu's summer morning beyond the canopy of the pilot's cockpit.

"Fossil's waiting for the workers' shift to change. If we take off when the night crew is docking and the next crew is on their way out, it'll look like we're part of the mining operation. In case there's anyone watching us who wonders why we never send all our ships out to the ice at the same time . . ."

Paige said, her voice as calm as always, "It's worth the wait. We don't seem to have picked up any trackers in that battle, but we sure don't want to give anyone who might be watching something suspicious to report."

Spennie slapped her cards down, too. "It can't be much longer now. I'm going to get strapped in. Rose, want me to patch you in to my recording for the trip out? It's an old Five Sabers Classic Cup."

For a moment Rose was tempted by the distraction. Then she glanced at Paige, her self-assured, cool-tempered pilot/gunner of a big sister—and recognized disappointment in the wry, sad little smile twisting at the corner of Paige's mouth.

Rose knew what her sister was thinking. Paige had been looking forward to their hour alone in the gunner's ball turret in the quiet blue of hyperspace.

"Thanks," Rose said. "But I'll be okay." She added lightly, "The trip out is our family time."

Cobalt Squadron cleared hyperspace as close to the Atterra Belt as was safe so that they could swing in among the asteroids quickly. The plan was to lurk there in the cover of the maze as long as possible and then venture out in pairs.

There were two swarms of TIE fighters glittering on Rose's tech screen when *Hammer* reached the inner edge of the Atterra Belt.

"Track along the asteroids so we come into orbit on Bravo's dark side," Rose warned the pilot.

"What are you, my flight instructor?" Finch quipped. "Of course I'm doing that."

The TIEs swarmed past like a meteor shower across the top and bottom corners of the monitor, fading off into the darkness on their patrol assignment. They were definitely expecting the heavy bombers to come back, but they hadn't spotted them yet.

"Cobalt *Belle*, are you with us?" called Finch.

Hammer's crew held their breath as they waited for the

response they couldn't hear. Then they heard Finch's confirmation of that response:

"All right. We'll be entering Bravo's orbit at three-five-oh. Watch for us. Don't head in until we've attracted some fire. Then race to the drop point from the other direction. When you've finished, come and join us for the fun."

For the benefit of *Hammer*'s crew, Finch repeated the *Belle* pilot's reply.

"*Belle* says they *can't wait* to join the fun."

————

Hammer's bomb bays were empty.

The bomber was as light and maneuverable as it was possible for a StarFortress to be. Finch had flown a couple of tight turns on the way out just to prove it. Now they were sailing into the sun over Atterra Bravo's daylight side, avoiding the brightly winking mines reflecting sunlight, *daring* the enemy to come chasing after them.

Meanwhile, the bomber Cobalt *Belle* was heading through Atterra Bravo's night toward the second drop point—the one they'd failed to reach two days earlier. It was a once-busy spaceport on the largest of the Firestone Islands. Like the location of the first drop, it was now an abandoned ruin, but it was accessible by makeshift ground transport for the planet's inhabitants.

Now that Rose was part of the team that was supposed

to distract the enemy from the Resistance bombers' real purpose, she found herself furious that the TIEs hadn't reappeared on her screen.

Come on, come on, you evil little space bugs, she thought at them. *COME ON. We're ready for you this time. . . .*

She shouldn't have worried. Of course they came back.

This chase was completely different from the one that had devastated Cobalt Squadron two days earlier.

Seeing the enemy coming, *Hammer* managed to race a good distance away from the planet before the squadron of TIEs caught up.

Rose, at the flight engineer's monitor, shouted warnings to the gunners.

"Two more bandits coming in at oh-one-oh, high!"

It was reassuring to feel the answering cannon fire shuddering through the floor of the flight deck below her feet—and to see the occasional white spark wink out as one of the TIEs was hit.

It wasn't long before the outline of another StarFortress appeared on Rose's screen, emerging from around the edge of Atterra Bravo's dark side.

"*Belle*'s joining us!" she yelled at the rest of her crew.

"I heard!" Finch answered. "They just called in! Made the drop without any interference! Good to see you, *Belle*!"

The bomber *Belle*, as maneuverable as *Hammer* now

that it had shed its load, came streaking into the Atterran daylight with its laser cannons ablaze.

For a few minutes they fought together, back-to-back. Rose stopped thinking, stopped anticipating the next moment, stopped worrying even. She was entirely focused on her monitors and her warnings to Spennie and Paige in the gun turrets.

Then, suddenly, Finch yelled breathlessly, "*Mare* has made their drop. *Belle*, we're going to love you and leave you—you're on your own now."

The whole crew heard him laugh.

"What's so funny?" Paige called up.

"*Belle* told me to shut up and go home," Finch said.

He banked and shot forward toward the Atterra Belt, leaving *Mare* to join the battle with *Belle* while *Treasure* took its turn racing to the drop site in secret.

Rose jumped up from the monitors and ran to check the baffler. She wanted to be sure it was ready to hide their track as they wove among the asteroids. She could tell by the cannon fire coming from Spennie's turret that there were TIE fighters still on their tail.

There was a series of thuds against the bomber's hull as it encountered a handful of small asteroids on the edge of the belt. They bounced off the heavy bomber's armor plating. But the much smaller TIEs weren't so lucky. Rose saw bursts of light beyond the pilot's cockpit as the TIE fighters, overtaking the StarFortress, flew headlong into the invisible space debris and exploded.

"We did it! We did it!"

Paige hadn't waited for Rose to join her in the lower ball turret after the jump to hyperspace; the entire *Hammer* crew had raced for a reunion on the flight deck, hugging each other and exclaiming in relief and triumph.

"Okay, okay, cool down, kids. . . ." That was Finch, of course. Every now and then he took over from Paige the role of being the sensible one. "We did it and *Belle* and *Mare* did it, but we won't know until we get home whether they survived—or if *Treasure* and *Bolide* and *Dancer* will, too—"

"Yes, but it was *working*, the plan was *working*!" Paige was jubilant.

Spennie added, "And if we keep them guessing—"

"We only have two more runs to make!" Nix finished. He grabbed Rose in a bear hug. "Great work, tech!"

"Great work yourself!"

It didn't look as if any of them were going to calm down any time soon.

"Another card game?" Finch suggested. "Since we're all up here, anyway."

Nix sighed. "More virtual fathiers! That's not much of a celebration."

"I know! Let's have a picnic," said Paige, grinning.

And from somewhere within her flight suit, she pulled out a slim sealed protein box and pried it open. Inside lay ten thin slices of starberry, still moist and crisp—two slices each.

"I saved mine," she said. "I reckoned we'd either need to lift our spirits, or we'd have something to celebrate."

This time, Rose savored every bite.

They felt the blast in hyperspace. There was a cataclysmic jolt, as if the ship had hit a wall, and a shock of blinding white light blazed all around the heavy bomber as if it were flying through a planetary lightning storm.

But then the mottled peaceful blue resealed itself around them, and Rose could find nothing wrong with the ship apart from two cracked blast shields, which might have happened in the battle earlier. And they still seemed to be on course for Refnu.

It sobered up their mood, though.

They didn't realize the shock hadn't been connected to their own journey until they reentered realspace.

When they came back into realspace around Refnu, they found themselves surrounded by light. It flickered around the ship like a titanic electrical fault. But the light wasn't coming from Refnu's distant sun. There were strange cosmic shock waves reverberating across the distant reaches of the star system.

"What in the name of the galaxy is *that*?" Finch muttered as he set the coordinates for the local flight to Refnu. "It's messing with the electronics. I have to punch everything in four or five times before it takes."

Nix came to lean over Rose's shoulder as she scanned through the ship's confused data log, trying to figure out what was wrong. Everything seemed to be working—it was just *jarred*.

"It looks okay. . . ." Rose trailed off.

"What is going on in the sky?" Paige called up from the lower turret.

"Wow," was Spennie's only comment. *"Wow."*

Rose and Nix couldn't see a thing that they were able to do, so they went to stand behind Finch and watch the sky as he came into Refnu's orbit for landing. Paige joined them.

"That's the best light show I've ever seen," Nix commented.

"Can you feel it?" Paige asked. "Is it affecting flight?"

Finch shook his head slowly. He lifted his hands from the controls and offered them to Paige.

"Try it."

Paige leaned in over his shoulder, taking over from Finch for a moment. Then she shook her head, as well.

"No, I can't feel a thing, either. Weird. It looks so *big*."

"If it's from outside this system, then maybe it's old light," Nix said. "A supernova a million years ago—the light is just arriving now. That's why we don't feel it, maybe."

"We *did* feel it," said Rose. "We felt it in hyperspace."

"Rose is right," said Finch slowly. "Also . . . it's messing with the electronics, even if it's not affecting our flying. I don't think the light is from outside this system. But the disturbance might be."

"Are you kidding?" said Paige sharply. "It'd have to be traveling faster than lightspeed. What could have happened that would make shock waves travel *that fast*?"

"I don't know," Finch answered. "Some kind of electronic disturbance, particle displacement, maybe—things suddenly shifted where they shouldn't be. Space lightning. I don't know."

He added soberly, "And I'm not sure I want to."

For once, the inhabitants of Refnu were gathered outside. The wharfs and windy wastes of the twilit landscape were crowded as people emerged from the tunnels and stared up at the sky.

One by one, the rest of the Resistance heavy bombers came back to the wharf. Every one of them had successfully made its airlift drop on Atterra Bravo, and only two had been superficially damaged in combat with the TIE fighters as they held up their end of the defensive strategy.

The transport also came back from D'Qar with fuel and a cargo of refilled clips and airlift supplies for the last two hops.

The *Hammer* crew had expected an exuberant debriefing, but the strange shock to the galaxy had sobered the entire squadron.

"You *all* felt the disruption?" Fossil asked again, in disbelief. "You all felt it during the journey through *hyperspace*?"

Everyone nodded.

"We felt it, too," said the captain of the transport. "Like hitting a wall. Like a—a disruption in the space-time continuum, like a disruption in . . ."

The transport pilot left his sentence hanging, but Rose thought that everyone there must know what he was thinking: *a disruption in the Force.*

They'd all heard the stories of how the Death Star had blown up an entire world, General Leia Organa's homeworld of Alderaan, in the last years of the Empire. But that had been before most of the bomber squadron crews were born, and the galaxy was essentially at peace now, apart from the rumblings of the First Order as they stretched for sovereignty among the Outer Rim and the independent star systems. And not even the destruction of a planet would have such a stunning and far-reaching impact on the rest of the galaxy. Everyone knew that an old star exploded now and then somewhere across the vast distances of the universe. It didn't produce a shock like this.

What had happened?

"Supernova," Rose heard a lot of people muttering.

"Supernova. That's the only thing that makes sense."

"What if it's some kind of weapon, though?"

"No way."

"Nothing could be that *big*."

"Who'd use something that big, anyway?"

"Supernova. Has to be."

Rose noticed that Casca Panzoro sat silent throughout the heated discussion in the debriefing room. She wondered what Casca was thinking. No one had mentioned calling off the last two hops to Atterra Bravo, but Rose thought that Casca must be worried about it. And worried about her grandson, with whom she had no hope of communicating.

Paige leaned over to Rose and whispered, "Ready for anything, right?"

"Yes, but I like to know what's going on," Rose whispered back. "I'm not such a fan of unexplained galactic super-explosions."

"Nothing's changed for the Atterra run," Paige assured her.

But something did change.

There were no TIE fighters waiting for them on the next day's airlift.

The six Resistance heavy bombers met with clear and empty space all across the Atterra system.

"It's too quiet," Finch growled, flying smoothly out of Atterra's daylight, leaving *Cutter* to be met by *Hailstorm* as backup while *Treasure* made its drop.

"Stop complaining," Paige called calmly up from the lower gun turret. "You sound like Rose."

"It's nice to have nothing to do up here for once," said Spennie from the tail gunner's turret.

"It's like they're *planning* something," Finch said.

"No," Rose said. "It's like they've flown the coop. It's like the patrols have all been called away to deal with something else, and there's nothing left of the blockade but the minefield and the automatic cannons in the belt. As if . . ."

"As if a few supply runs to a star system already under

their control don't really matter to the First Order any-more?" suggested Nix. "After all that fighting to keep us out, why would they suddenly stop caring?"

"Maybe they've got a bigger fight on their hands some-where else," said Spennie.

"Or maybe," said Paige quietly, "the rumors about the *weapon* aren't just rumors. Maybe the First Order thinks they've got a weapon that's so big they don't need to worry about a few heavy bombers."

15

*H*AMMER HAD a different role to play in the final supply drop. It was landing on Atterra Bravo to take Casca Panzoro back to her people on the Firestone Islands.

Paige, who'd flown in to Atterra Bravo before and had a little experience with its climate and geography, was going to do the piloting. Finch flew as tail gunner so they were both on the flight deck in case Paige needed to consult with him. Spennie took over Paige's seat in the lower gun turret. Meanwhile, *Hammer*'s bomb racks were stocked with supplies that would be unloaded once they were on the surface of the planet.

Rose sat on the floor by Paige's feet while they sailed through hyperspace. She was self-conscious about sharing Paige's seat as she'd have done in the lower gun turret, because both Nix and Casca were riding on the flight deck with them. Having Casca aboard changed the whole dynamic of *Hammer*'s crew. They were all a little more polite, a little more well-behaved than usual.

It made Rose feel faintly as if she wanted to pick a fight with someone. She was possessive of the quiet, familiar hyperspace time that she was used to sharing with her sister.

Everything was different on this last trip.

"How long to realspace?" Rose asked. She wanted to get this particular drop over with—dropping a *person* seemed much more complicated than dropping shells. But Fossil had insisted that they not risk the attention of launching Casca from an escape pod—or the possibility of landing her in the acid sea—and Casca couldn't pilot a shuttle. So that meant she had to be delivered in one of the bombers themselves. And of course *Hammer*'s crew had volunteered.

"Realspace? Half an hour."

"No picnic today?"

"Seems like the celebration ought to wait for the journey home," said Paige. "Don't want to lull ourselves into a false sense of security. I always kind of feel that way on the last assignment of a mission, you know? Like we've become invulnerable. If the worst hasn't already happened, it can't possibly happen *now*."

Rose fingered her Otomok medallion, thinking of Cat. "Or—the worst has already happened. It can't possibly happen *again*."

"Or," Paige said, "the worst is still to come. But it's not going to happen *today.*"

"You're sounding like me again," Rose teased.

"Full of gloom?" Paige laughed softly. "Well . . . I'm optimistic about this hop."

She glanced over at Casca Panzoro, sitting with her knees drawn up and her back against the ducts lining the wall of the fuselage, just as she'd sat when *Hammer* had first picked her up with her grandson, Reeve, in their desperate escape from Atterra Bravo not much more than a week before. Casca's eyes were closed. She'd taken off her headset. Her hands moved gracefully as she recited some private prayer or recitation.

Rose couldn't imagine being that unselfconscious. But then, neither could she imagine being district representative of anything. She couldn't imagine *commanding* people.

She tried to imagine it—and realized that she'd just spent a week giving commands to all the flight engineers of Cobalt Squadron and half of Crimson.

Rose laughed at herself. When Casca looked up, Rose gave her a friendly smile.

Paige followed Rose's gaze. "Casca's grateful," Paige said softly. "More grateful than any of us can understand, I think. And that gives me *hope.*"

She paused. Into her moment's silence, Rose prompted, trying to make Paige laugh: "But you don't like her hair? Or what?"

Paige only smiled. She shook her head.

"I'm glad we've helped Atterra Bravo, and I know we might have made a difference. I hope they win their battle. At the very least, we've collected some solid evidence for Leia's case against the First Order—those death transports, and the number of starfighters that have been attacking us without even knowing what our business is. . . . But I'm worried. Whatever happened yesterday . . . I don't know what it was. I'm worried that everything we've done this week is just too late. That there's something else going on that is just . . . more *important* than what we've done this week. That Otomok and Atterra aren't any more significant than *Wasp* and *Scarab* and *Hornet* . . . and it won't matter if we help Atterra or not—"

"You're scaring me," Rose interrupted.

Paige stopped abruptly. She gave Rose another half smile.

"Don't be scared. We're still alive and we're still together. And we're doing what we can," Paige said, resuming her ordinary precombat calm. "Let's hope our last run goes as smoothly as yesterday's did."

————

This time *Belle* was the maneuverable StarFortress, the empty one carrying no weighty shells. While *Hammer* headed toward the Firestone Islands in Atterra Bravo's nighttime orbit, *Belle* flew out of the asteroid maze and into Atterra Bravo's daylight ahead of the other bombers as a decoy. Behind *Hammer, Mare* came in for a drop elsewhere in the Firestones.

Rose and Casca both came to stand behind Paige as she lowered *Hammer* close to the ground in the utter darkness near the Big Settlement on Firestone Island.

They'd had no way of contacting the Atterrans ahead of time to let them know what was going on. And they hadn't planned Casca's return in advance, which meant that the Big Settlement wasn't expecting them. There was no place to dock the top-heavy ship on the pumice beach, so Finch told Paige to set the engines to hover; they'd have to tether the ship a little above the ground and climb out through the bomb bay access hatch.

There wasn't a single light visible, no more than there'd been on any of *Hammer*'s previous trips to Atterra Bravo. The landscape seemed so desolate and defeated that, as the StarFortress set down and Paige lowered the power, Rose felt a kind of dread rising in her. What if this really had all been for nothing? What if everyone on the island was already dead? What if they were delivering Casca

Panzoro home to a lifeless and deserted planet with no water?

In the bomb bay below, Nix opened the outer hatch and threw out the self-fixing tethering cables. Paige and Finch guided Casca down the bomb bay ladder.

"You're going to have to rally some bodies to help unload these racks," Nix told Casca. "Or else we'll have to take off again and jettison them for your people to collect later. We can't do it ourselves."

"We'll wake the Big Settlement," Casca said. "We're used to working in the dark."

She emerged from the hatch and swung down onto the windy, chemical-scented porous stone beach. Nix, Rose, and Paige climbed out behind her.

The air around them suddenly whistled with the flight of dozens of small missiles, invisible in the darkness, that hissed and sizzled as they struck the tethering cables and the foot of the heavy bomber. Rose remembered the solar crossbow she'd seen the old man aiming at her, and at Paige and Reeve, when they'd first arrived in the Big Settlement.

"Don't shoot!" Casca yelled. *"Stop—it's Casca Panzoro!"*

Rose felt a searing jolt of electricity crackling across her arm, just for a second. One of the charged arrows had glanced off her flight suit. When she looked down, a patch of her singed sleeve glowed with tiny orange sparks—the only light she could see on the dark surface of Atterra Bravo.

Paige grabbed Rose's arm with both hands, smothering the sparks as quickly as they'd ignited.

Paige and Casca yelled into the dark together. *"Bravo Rising! We're the airlift! Don't shoot!"*

"Don't shoot!" echoed a young man's voice from the darkness of the pumice beach, in such firm tones of command that the whistling and thudding stopped instantly.

"Are you hurt?" Paige asked frantically, with one arm around Rose as if she was trying to support her while she ran the other hand up and down Rose's arm checking for damage.

"I don't think so," Rose answered. "The bolt just grazed the outside of my flight suit. I wasn't going to be wearing it to an embassy dinner anyway. It's *okay*, Paige!"

Rose couldn't remember her sister being this upset since they'd left Otomok.

"I felt the shock, but I can't feel a hole in my sleeve," Rose said. "I'm not hurt!"

Dark figures came forward in the starlight. Voices babbled apologies.

"We can't tell the ships apart in the dark. The First Order has been circling the planet, too—"

"And then there was the explosion yesterday—"

"Explosion?" Someone spoke over the top of the other

speaker. "That wasn't an explosion. That was some kind of solar flare—"

The Atterrans of the Firestone Islands were just as ferociously on edge as everyone else who'd felt the strange shock waves reverberating through the galaxy the day before.

Hammer's crew couldn't give them any more of an explanation than what they were inventing on their own. Finch, emerging behind the rest of them, didn't even try. He just skipped straight to what they had in common. "Are the drops getting through?" he asked.

A slight, youthful figure stepped forward in the dark and answered firmly in a clear voice, "Thank you, thank you! Yes. We've picked up all three of them. The reason we're out on foot tonight is because we were hoping to get to the final drop before dawn."

"Is that *Reeve*?" cried Paige and Casca together.

Suddenly, the district representative and her pilot grandson were locked in a desperate embrace, while Paige clung to Rose.

After Casca had let go of Reeve, he whirled spontaneously and threw his arms around both Paige and Rose at the same time. Then he stepped back, trying to see them clearly, but the night was too dark for any of them to see much more than shadows.

"I'd have stopped people from shooting at you sooner if we'd been able to see your ship," Reeve exclaimed. "I'd know that heavy bomber anywhere!"

"Was that *you* telling them to stop?" Rose asked. There had been no sign of fear in that command. "Wow, getting into action sure has changed you—you're the head of Bravo Rising now!"

"Well, I'm glad Ms. Casca's here to take over," Reeve said. "I don't like the responsibility! But it's good to know I can do it if I have to. It wasn't just getting into action that helped. It's knowing that people trust me. And also . . ." He hesitated.

"A dash of hope?" suggested Paige.

"I thought Rose would think it was corny if I said that."

"It is corny." Rose laughed. "But probably true."

"Thank you for giving me hope," said Reeve. "For giving *us* hope."

Finch cleared his throat and rapped his blaster against the tethering cable that held down the StarFortress. The sound rang clearly over everybody's voices and the never-ending sound of the acidic surf at the edge of the beach.

"I think we need to pull this meeting together," Finch announced. "We can't stay long. How's your night vision, folks? We're going to have to unload this crate in the dark."

He climbed back up through the hatch behind Nix to

help the bombardier open the bomb bay doors and release the supply canisters for unloading. Then he called back out to Paige.

"Get up there in the cockpit and get ready to boost the power. I want this ship off the ground the second the bomb bay doors are shut again." He drew a long, suspicious breath. "I don't like the way this place smells."

"Come on up with me, Rose," Paige said. "And Reeve: keep up the good work."

They clasped and squeezed each other's hands in the dark, exchanging good-byes with Reeve and Casca.

The power baffler chirped a friendly greeting at Rose as she climbed up onto the flight deck.

"Little monster, you're the best," she told it fondly. *Hammer* had made the trip from Refnu to Atterra five times, in addition to the first trip from D'Qar, and the power baffler had only failed her once. Rose was proud of it.

Paige set the power. Rose felt the low hum through her feet in the dark.

"Hey, *Hammer*, how's it going?" came the voice of *Bolide*'s pilot through the general comm system. "All's well up here. We just made our drop and we're heading out to relieve *Dancer*. *Belle* last reported in just before it jumped to lightspeed, and *Mare* and *Treasure* are on their way through the asteroid belt. You're the last."

"Any action?"

"Just one patrol of TIEs. They didn't stick around, either. I don't know what's going on and I don't like it, but this is our last hop, so I'm not going to worry about it."

"Don't wait for us. If it's that quiet, we'll make our own way out of here," Paige told them. "Be careful of the mine-fields. See you back on Refnu!"

"Stay safe," *Bolide*'s pilot called in farewell, and checked out.

Rose gave a snort. "He's too embarrassed to say, 'May the Force be with you.' He doesn't believe in it."

Paige shook her head.

"Not everybody does."

She turned to Rose. "Are you sure you're okay?"

"Sure I'm sure!"

"I can't believe you made it through this whole mission without getting blown up, and then some kid with a blow-gun on a planet that can't even produce its own water tries to shoot your arm off." Paige's voice shook a little.

"Come on, Paige, it didn't even damage my elegant eveningwear! And it's not like you to make a fuss—"

"I wouldn't if it had happened to me. But it happened to *you*. And I'm supposed to take care of you."

Rose was silent for a minute. They sat in the dark,

waiting for the people working below them to finish unloading the ship.

Then Rose said to her sister, "You know who's been the bravest person involved in this whole operation?"

Paige didn't answer. Rose wondered if her sister guessed what she was going to say.

"I thought Reeve was pretty brave when he came with us on that first reconnaissance trip," Rose said, "flying across the Outer Rim all by himself with strangers."

"You didn't even want to fly with him because he was so scared of everything!"

Rose laughed. "He *was* scared. It didn't stop him, though. He did what he had to do anyway. He helped us escape that First Order patrol ship. He probably saved our lives by grabbing up that water bottle that I dropped. And then he decided to stay on Atterra Bravo when we left."

Paige laughed. "But? I always know when there's going to be a 'but.'"

"But Casca Panzoro is a million times braver. She had to let Reeve go."

"Yes," Paige agreed softly. "Yes, she is. . . ."

It was Rose's turn to laugh. "But?"

"Going on separate missions was brave of them," Paige said. "But it was really nice seeing them get back together again."

———

Of all the people who could have been waiting to meet the bomber crews when they struggled out of their Refnu weathersuits in the debriefing room after their last hop to Atterra, Rose did not expect Vice-Admiral Amilyn Holdo of the Resistance cruiser *Ninka*.

That night the look in her eyes was wintry. She didn't greet anyone aloud as they filed past her into the room, but Rose could see that she was watching and noting each crew member individually, assessing their enthusiasm and their exhaustion. In Rose's case, the singed sleeve got a nod. When everyone was gathered together and Fossil stood waiting at the front of the room, Holdo strode to meet her and addressed the Cobalt and Crimson Squadrons.

"Thank you for"—Holdo paused, looking around the room, catching individual eyes—"for *everything* you've done this week."

She looked at Fossil. "Thank you, Commander."

Fossil nodded, blinking her enormous eyes. Holdo turned back to the gathered StarFortress crews.

"I've heard from Fossil all that's happened," she said. "And I want to give you time to rest, to recover from wounds, to address your grief. I want to hear every individual report and impression. But I can't do any of that. We've no time for it. You're aware of the stellar shock of two days ago?"

They all nodded silently.

"It was a First Order attack on Hosnian Prime. It was an attack that *destroyed* the Hosnian star system." She paused again, to let that sink in. "It destroyed *the entire system.*"

It was almost too enormous to comprehend.

And yet, nothing short of the destruction of an entire star system could explain the disturbance to the galaxy that they'd all witnessed.

Someone raised a hand and ventured, "How—?"

"The astonishing weapon they constructed has already been destroyed, as well," Holdo said grimly. "It happened *today.* You, like me and my ship, were too far away to lend your aid. In any case, before the First Order could draw down the starpower to use their weapon a second time, the Resistance met them and stopped them. But the result of their attack on Hosnian Prime, and of our Resistance retaliation, is that we are now openly at war with the First Order."

Rose heard quiet gasps around the room.

Paige reached for her hand and squeezed. Rose glanced at her sister. Paige's face was drained, but her expression was calm as always.

And, as always, Rose could guess what she was thinking.

It was a relief to have this out in the open—to know that their fight would be in daylight now. That Atterra's fight would be supported. That anyone who had escaped from Otomok would be believed.

But it was a bitter satisfaction.

"You've served the Resistance loyally on this mission. You've seen your comrades die. You must move on to the next battle without regret," Holdo said. "Don't spend time dwelling on the past. Look forward now. Dedicate yourselves to creating the best possible future."

It hardly seemed possible that Holdo could find some positive encouragement for them under the circumstances, but Rose clung to every word.

"General Leia Organa has initiated an evacuation of the D'Qar base," Holdo finished. "There's no doubt our security has been breached. We need you, the heavy bombers, to return with me and the *Ninka*. We need you armed and able to fight in defense of the evacuation. Who is ready and willing?"

Every arm in the room shot up. Paige and Rose, still holding tight to each other's hands where they sat side by side among the assembled crew members, raised opposite arms.

Holdo was silent for a moment, moved.

Fossil nodded again and said, "We are at your command."

"My cruiser can provide you with armament," Holdo told the bomber crews. "We'll help you load the bomb racks. Fossil tells me you have enough crew for two squadrons of four bombers. You'll fly as the Cobalt Squadron and the Crimson Squadron as usual. We can provide a starfighter escort of twenty X- and A-wings. Kaiden, Zanyo, Vennie?"

Holdo turned to each as she spoke their names. "I'd like to put the three of you back in starfighters. The rest of you must redistribute your crews. Rose Tico?"

Rose found Vice-Admiral Holdo looking her directly in the eyes. "I'd like you to come on board the *Ninka* as part of our maintenance team. We're desperately short of good technicians, and I'm afraid we've got a bitter fight ahead of us. I'm impressed with the work you've done this week; you're quick and reliable and you're good at taking orders, as well as at taking initiative. I need you on my ship."

Paige squeezed Rose's hand.

It was an encouraging squeeze. It said: *Go on. Now's your chance.*

If Rose went with Holdo, she would have to fly without Paige for the first time.

We are now openly at war with the First Order, Holdo had said. *I need you on my ship.*

Rose thought of Reeve Panzoro, and the decision he'd made when Bravo Rising had told him how desperately they needed him to stay on Atterra Bravo. Rose remembered how easily she'd imagined Reeve's thoughts: *Ms. Casca's the only one I have left. If I do this, I might never see her again.*

She couldn't help thinking the same thing now, about Paige.

But she also remembered Reeve's words: *She'd want me to do the job I was needed for. So would my father.*

And how Paige had answered him: *Well, then. There you go.*

"We'll reshuffle everybody after the evacuation," Holdo promised, seeing Rose's hesitation. "All right?"

Rose swallowed. Then, suddenly, she gave a sharp nod.

She let go of Paige's hand.

She knew that now she was going to be able to navigate new uncharted stars alone.

"All right," said Rose. "I'll do it."

———

The cruiser *Ninka* hovered overhead while work crews shuttled out for boarding. The *Ninka* was too large to dock at the wharf where the bombers were berthed, and Rose was scheduled for the shuttle after the next. For a few more minutes, though, she crowded up against her sister in the lower gun turret of the Cobalt bomber *Hammer*.

Outside, instead of the quiet blue of hyperspace, the Refnu docks were busy with people running back and forth, handing over rented weathersuits, finishing the refueling process, and loading bomb clips. Rose had just finished dismantling *Hammer's* baffler and was checking to make sure that Paige's cannons were working.

But it gave her an excuse to steal five minutes alone with her big sister.

"What made you decide to say yes?" Paige asked.

"I wanted a new flight suit," Rose said.

Paige gave a little laugh, just as Rose had hoped she would. Then Rose tried to explain the truth.

"I kept thinking about Reeve Panzoro. Being brave. Taking responsibility. The outbreak of war. And then you squeezing my hand, encouraging me." Rose fiddled with the Otomok medallion around her neck. "Lots of things."

She felt suddenly anxious. "I thought you wanted me to," she said. "I thought you were ready to let me take responsibility for *myself*."

"I want you to be yourself," said Paige. "But of course that means being my sister, too."

Paige had her own Otomok medallion wrapped around the gunsight mount of the cannon, as she often did, but now she untied it and hung it back around her neck, the way Rose was wearing hers.

"Nothing can change that," said Paige. "We're connected to each other, and to home. We don't have to be in the same place for that to be true."

"I know it, Pae-Pae," said Rose.

"You goof." Paige hugged her fondly. "You'd better go. You've got to return that weathersuit before you board the shuttle."

"Okay." Rose gave her sister one last hug. "See you after the evacuation."

"See you then, Rose," said Paige.

Rose climbed out of the gun turret, and out of the bomb bay access hatch. From outside the ship, she could still see Paige in the clear crystal sphere of the ball turret, smiling and waving.

Rose waved back. *See you then.*

ACKNOWLEDGMENTS

With special thanks to Kristin Rens for being so patient. Thanks also to Harry Genge for his list of names, and to the Canadian Warplane Heritage Museum for the fabulous flight in their Lancaster bomber.